MARIA INÉS

MARIA INÉS

A NOVEL

ANNE SCHROEDER

FIVE STAR
A part of Gale, Cengage Learning

GALE
CENGAGE Learning·

Farmington Hills, Mich • San Francisco • New York • Waterville, Maine
Meriden, Conn • Mason, Ohio • Chicago

GALE
CENGAGE Learning·

LIBRARY OF CONGRESS CATALOGING-IN-PUBLICATION DATA

Names: Schroeder, Anne, 1948– author.
Title: Maria Inés : a novel / Anne Schroeder.
Description: Waterville, Maine : Five Star, a part of Cengage Learning, Inc.
Identifiers: LCCN 2016007345 (print) | LCCN 2016011733 (ebook) | ISBN 9781432832773 (hardcover) | ISBN 1432832778 (hardcover) | ISBN 9781432832711 (ebook) | ISBN 1432832719 (ebook) | ISBN 9781432833480 (ebook) | ISBN 1432833480 (ebook)
Subjects: LCSH: Girls—California—Fiction. | Group identity—Fiction. | Identity (Psychology)—Fiction. | California—History—19th century—Fiction | GSAFD: Historical fiction.
Classification: LCC PS3619.C46463 M37 2016 (print) | LCC PS3619.C46463 (ebook) | DDC 813/.6—dc23
LC record available at http://lccn.loc.gov/2016007345

First Edition. First Printing: October 2016
Find us on Facebook– https://www.facebook.com/FiveStarCengage
Visit our website– http://www.gale.cengage.com/fivestar/
Contact Five Star™ Publishing at FiveStar@cengage.com

Printed in the United States of America
1 2 3 4 5 6 7 20 19 18 17 16

To the Salinan people as they regain their cultural identity.

ACKNOWLEDGMENTS

This story is the result of so many good and generous people:

My husband, for his encouragement and tire tread as he shared the research.

Rob Natiuk, for helping me find my narrative voice and offering substantive edits.

Bradd Hopkins for cinematic suggestions.

John Warner, Salinan music expert and docent at San Miguel.

Dan Krieger, Professor Emeritus history at Cal Poly.

Liz Krieger, for her encouragement.

Jan Potter, California history expert and docent at Mission San Luis Obispo.

Hazel Rumney and Erin Bealmear, Editors at Five Star Publishing.

Joyce Herman, Friends of the Adobe, for reading the uncompleted novel.

Dawn Dunlap, Cambria rancher and sister member of Native Daughters of the Golden West.

Salinan tribal members Susan Latta and Suzanne Pierce Taylor for reading and commenting on the work-in-progress.

The docents of Missions San Miguel, San Antonio, and San Luis Obispo, the Museums at Morro Bay, San Lorenzo Park in King City, and the people who support these centers.

Acknowledgments

The many local writers who have published, many times at their own expense, their research and family stories.

History belongs to each of us. We each have an obligation to write our stories so that others may know our journey.

GLOSSARY OF SALINAN WORDS

Ama'—The man's father; paternal grandfather.

a p'xa—Child.

Hianisponica—A Salinan prayer word for God.

Ku-ku-su—Owl Dance.

Lyrics: "pa'-na-ta, pa'-na-ta, co'ko-nai" Dance, dance, owl.

Kuksu'I—Bear Dance.

Lyrics: "hau'-wa-ya," there's plenty. "he'-ne-ye," we are glad. "hau'-wa-ya, he'-ne-ye, he'-ne-ye." There's plenty, we are glad, we are glad, we are glad.

Le Sa Mo—A sacred place of beginning at Morro Rock in the harbor of Morro Bay.

NenE'—The woman's parents.

Oxwe't—(Yokut language) The man's mother; paternal grandmother.

pek—One.

pek-walanai—Six.

pemaxala—Five.

peu—Hide and seek game played like soccer across vast areas; game includes betting.

pooish—Sacrifice and homage paid to the pagan god, Cooksuy, that continued for many Indians even after their Christianization.

Sepxá—The white God.

shaamo'sh—Greeting of welcome.

t'a'a'u'—Fire.

ta· xwe'ne' or t'axwe'n'—Dove.

T'e Lxo—Thunder.

TopE—Trinket basket.

ts'a-kai—Wind.

tule—A fibrous reed growing near the river.

Ta ta' or e'pex—Father.

xamaxus—Four.

xulax—Two.

xulax-walanai—Seven.

xulep—Three.

YaHa—Expression of good humor.

The Lord's Prayer—"Za til i, mo quixco nepe limaatnil. An zucueteyem na etsmatz; antsiejtsitia na ejtamilina an citaha natsmalog zui lac quicha nepe lima." (Our Father who art in Heaven, hallowed be thy name. Thy kingdom come, thy will be done on earth as it is in Heaven.)

GLOSSARY OF SPANISH WORDS USED IN THE CONTEXT OF THE CALIFORNIA MISSION ERA

Alcalde—For the Spanish people, a mayor or judge of a pueblo or village, appointed by the governor. At the missions, Indian alcaldes were appointed by the padre as policemen, and were supplied with stockings and shoes to distinguish them.

Antoniaños—Northern Salinan Indians living at Mission San Antonio de Padua.

Asistencia—Grain storage building of adobe and rock built a distance from Mission San Luis Obispo de Tolosa.

Atole—A subsistence soup made of corn served to neophytes.

Baile—A formal dance or ball.

Bandidos—Often disenfranchised gentry or ship deserters, who terrorized travelers on El Camino Real after the American takeover of California.

Bota—leather sacks for food and beverage storage.

Caballeros—Sons of Spanish or Mexican families known for their horsemanship skills.

Cacique—Indian in charge of punishment at the Missions.

Calabozo—Room used as a jail at the Missions.

Carrera de gallo—Game of skill where a mounted rider at a full run pulls a rooster buried to its neck from the sand.

Carretas—Two-wheel oxcarts used to transport women and children, the infirm, and supplies.

Cholo—Derogative term for men of mixed Indian and Mexican heritage, often bandits.

Commadante—Military leader of the Mission guard.

Diablo—Devil of native superstition and Catholic teaching.

Documento—Scrap of rawhide on which an Indian's deed of ownership was recorded after the secularization of the Missions.

Dulce—Candy and sweets served to visitors and worthy neophytes on church feast days.

Embarazada—Pregnant.

El Camino Real—Literally "The King's Highway," today's U.S. Highway 101.

Escolte—The military guard assigned to protect each Mission and retrieve runaway Indians.

Fanega—A grain measure equal to 1.58 bushels.

Gente de razón—Literally "people of reason." Spanish citizens.

Grasa—Meat fat highly prized by protein-starved Indians.

Hechiceros—Wizards of Salinan religious legend.

Hectare—A measurement of land equal to approximately 100 acres.

Horno—Outdoor oven for baking bread usually served only to padres and visitors.

Majordomo—Indian labor foreman.

Mal Galico—The rotting disease; syphilis.

Mano—Grinding stone shaped like a rolling pin.

Masa—Ground corn used in tortillas.

Mas o menos—More or less. Land boundaries were approximate in a land of excess.

Matanza—A time designated by the padre for slaughtering cattle for skins for trading.

Metate—A grinding rock for corn or acorns.

Miguelaños—Salinan Indians living at Mission San Miguel de Arcángel.

Monjerio—Separate building with a courtyard and high walls where unmarried neophyte girls and young widows lived apart from male contact.

Morro—Rock. Morro Rock at Morro Bay is the traditional origin of the Salinan.

Neophyte—Christianized Indian workers.

Nuqueuadores—Specially trained Indians who killed the cattle by blunt force.

Ojo de Dios—Stylized eye representing God's all-seeing nature.

Olivella shells—Small seashells strung and used as money until the padres introduced colored glass beads from Europe.

Osos—Bear, specifically the both feared and revered grizzly.

Peladores—Indians trained to skin the slaughtered cattle.

Playaños—Salinan Indians living near the Pacific Ocean.

Pinos—Pine trees, a major source of food, medicine, and basket material.

Pozole—A porridge or thick soup of roasted wheat or barley, corn, beans, and bits of horsemeat, mutton or beef.

Ranchería—Spanish name for a Salinan Indian village.

Señor, Señora—Forms of address for Spanish or Mexican men and married women, as Mr. and Mrs.

Señorita—An unmarried Spanish or Mexican girl or woman.

Soldado—Spanish or Mexican soldier.

Soldados de cuero—Soldiers of the mission guard who wore leather jackets to protect themselves from arrows.

Sonoreños—Mexican citizens from Sonora who immigrated with hopes of free land.

Tasejeras—Indians trained to butcher the slaughtered cattle into strips for jerky.

Tulareños—Yokut Indians whose tribal land was in the Central Valley of California.

Yanqui—A derogative term for the American conquerors who were often lawless, unsuccessful gold miners.

CHAPTER ONE:
ALTA CALIFORNIA,
SEPTEMBER, 1818

The fury of the storm seemed to be a warning. The few who still called themselves the People of the Oaks whispered that the flooding was the gods' anger because they had left their villages and their traditional ways to dwell among the padres at Mission San Miguel Arcángel. But others argued not. For them the rain was a blessing from the true God.

"Let the rains come," a young woman prayed as she lay waiting for her next birthing pain. "Let us be safe this night." She was a *neophyte*, a baptized Indian with a name given to her by the padres and she felt afraid in this new place. But no travelers would arrive seeking hospitality in this weather. Tonight *El Camino Real* was flooded, the thin wagon track that followed the rivers and valleys from the border of New Spain, north to the Missions of Alta California. "Let the rains come," she repeated. "Let our fields and our hearts be renewed."

Her heart was one with the forces raging outside her walls, ancient winds whipping through the olive grove, ripping off branches and pitching them into the north wall of the dormitory. The sound of singers and cantors in the nearby church were muted as whorls of rain lashed the clay-tiled roofs, windows, and rough-hewn doors.

Alfonsa lay inside the adobe room assigned to her husband, Domingo. Restlessly, she stirred in her birthing bed, feeling its sturdy willow frame flex beneath her. A fragrant layer of pine needles sent out a sweet fragrance, sap freed by a layer of heated rocks in the trench beneath her. She breathed deeply and her mind saw the forest where, a few days earlier, she had walked from sunrise to sunset to gather pine boughs. Domingo had built the bed in the way of her ancestors to please her, a deep rectangular trench dug into in the hard-packed adobe floor holding five rocks still hot from the fire. His mother bound the frame with woven *tule* grass to protect the skin from the heat. Alfonsa now rested safely above the half-buried stones and waited.

"It is good, 'mingo," she whispered, and her heart swelled with gratitude. She longed to tell him this, but he was not present. His mother had chased him from the room because the old taboos did not allow him to take part in the birth. The two were both at evening service, along with every other neophyte, and she was alone.

A basket of pine nuts lay nearby, a gift he had brought so she would have strength for her ordeal. She glanced at the basket, but her body was filled with anticipation, not hunger—a thing her husband would not understand because his belly was never full, even after he had taken his meal. Alone but unafraid, she bit down on an olive twig to blunt her moan from the world outside. "The rain is God's gift," she whispered through cracked lips. "Our prayers are heard."

Another pain engulfed her. She shut her eyes, bit into the twig, and tried to hold onto yesterday's memory when Padre Juan Martin had stood in the courtyard, his hands raised to the sky as a warm breeze wafted his robe like the wings of a dove. Strong and fervent, his voice swelled to the cloudless sky as he led his people in prayer for rain. Rain so that there would be more wheat in the fields and vegetables in the gardens. Food for the *escolte*, the Spanish soldiers protecting the Mission. Food for the padres and their guests. Grain to trade to the other Missions and to send to the governor for taxes. And if there was any left, food for the neophytes, for her and her baby soon to be born.

The summer heat had been intense, the rain sparse, but the Spanish Governor de Solá had levied extra taxes in the form of wine and cattle hides. Many workers died in the latest round of hunger and typhoid, leaving fewer to gather the crops. She did not complain like some of the others who groused under their breath about the six hours of labor required of them—even though the padres worked as hard as any of them—but drought made things harder. Her belly, big with baby, made drawing water difficult; carrying the burden basket pulled down her shoulders and strained her back with the pressure of the strap. This is why she knew God had sent the rain for her, and just in time.

"Aiiiyaah." Another pain, this one harder. Her lips moved in the prayer of the Holy Mother who had given birth in a room no bigger than her own. Alfonsa swallowed her sob. "Hail Mary, mother of God . . ." She repeated the prayer that brought her strength in trial. Surely the Holy Virgin had shown courage at the birth of her son. *New life comes—blessing and pain.*

Across the room, the shadowy figure of an old woman swayed in prayer. Not the Latin chant of the padres and the choir, but in rhythm with the ancient people: prayers to the sun, moon, rain, golden eagle, as they had been prayed in the village of the spirit woman's childhood. Tonight, fire shadows danced on the wall. From a standing position, her old body swayed back and forth, translucent in the light of the flickering firelight, her ancient bones limber from a lifetime of sitting upon the earth. With almost every sway her forehead brushed the wall in front of her, allowing crushed limestone from the wall to mottle in the deep furrows of her forehead. Streaks of white caught in the strands of her hair, making her seem even grayer than the day she arrived. Her hair was long then, but she had singed it short with firebrands to show she mourned the loss of the old ways.

"Grandmother," Alfonsa whispered, "you've come." *NenE'*—the name the people called the mother of her mother. *NenE'*, the storyteller. In her dream, Grandmother told about *T'e Lxo*, the thunder. *T'e Lxo* roared from the sky in a dance with the lightning, and afterwards it was here, over this chosen valley and over her people, the stars would spread their blanket when the world was washed clean and the streams refilled.

Back and forth the old woman rocked. *Brish Brish.* Alfonsa knew she imagined it, so soft a sound, so soft a color, yet both stirred something deep inside her, a feeling that the old ways would never totally disappear. Grandmother was only here in spirit. She would be no help with the coming baby, but someone would arrive—maybe sooner, maybe later—when the common prayers in the church ended and the final meal of the day had been distributed.

A knotted rosary lay limp in Alfonsa's hand. Domingo had left her to her labor, but she listened for his footstep. Did not Saint Joseph wipe Mary's brow at the birthing of their son? *Ride the contraction as a wave,* the older mothers told her. But what did that mean?

Outside, the huge bells tolled against the crashing of the storm. Lightning flashed nearby, filling her room while thunder soon followed. A strong gust of wind blew through the cracks around the door, cooling her skin. Smoke stung her eyes as the intrusive wind fingered the fire in the corner.

She returned her gaze to Grandmother, who stood motionless, listening to the song of the wind. Did the wind tell the old one that her granddaughter would have a blessed and strong grandchild? In the woman's wrinkled face and sad eyes, strange secrets remained hidden from human understanding. Grandmother would know the meaning of the images that came during Alfonsa's own sleep, strange words that woke her when she cried out, sometimes with a few human words, but sometimes with the words of otherworld spirits. She wondered about the spirit world the elders no longer talked of, but it would do no good to ask. When she was a child she had questioned Padre Juan Cabot about them and he said the dead do not come back to the living. She left it at that. Padre should know these things, yet the belief did not leave her.

She felt the power of the river carrying her and her unborn child. In a moment of release from fierce pain, Alfonsa raised her arms. "My people," she sighed.

Another vision, one in which she gazed down from the starry blanket into the valley. She saw her people by the river, milling among their huts of *tule* grass bundled together with bark strips. So small, so simple. She found herself wailing in her dreaming. "Why can't I bring my baby into this world in a hut like my grandmother's? In my people's village? With the smell of grass and bark. With the songs of my people. Under the stars as *T'e Lxo* shouts from the sky."

Grandmother continued to rock on her toes and Alfonsa understood what was deep inside the old one's heart—fear. Fear for the baby about to be born.

"God help us," she whispered, her throat dry.

She managed a swallow of water from her drinking vessel, an abalone shell carried from the sandy beaches to the west. Suddenly the pungent scent of burning sage chased the sour smell of sweat and rancid grease from the tight, closed room. For this she was grateful, but not for the pagan smoke that would bring the wrath of Padre Martin upon them. She rose on her elbow and tried to fan the air away before the scent embedded itself in her hair and her skin.

"No, Grandmother, you must not. Padre says these things are of the devil. Superstition. You mustn't." Before she could prevent it, the old shadow woman managed to smudge her belly and her breasts, up to her chin with the black soot, her chants summoning the ancient spirits to provide for a strong baby, a safe birth. Spirits the old woman summoned were powerful. Alfonsa felt her body relaxing under the sweet cleansing. A moment later Grandmother's spirit faded and the room was empty.

A small sound issued from the doorway. It was *Oxwe't*, the mother of her husband, returning from the church. The shadowy image of Grandmother faded into darkness and the room was empty again except for the two of them. The new arrival wrinkled her nose and glanced around. A faint smile flickered over her customary frown.

Alfonsa felt the need to talk.

"*Oxwe't*, this room is built with skill and hard work. Your son honors us with his devotion." As she expected, the woman slipped to the floor without speaking. Domingo had explained to the padres that no Yokut woman would speak to her son's wife, not even if they passed in the field, but his pleading was dismissed like a mosquito's buzz. Padre claimed the old taboos were pagan. God required a man's wife to care for his aging mother.

His mother made a bed in the corner of the small room and said nothing unless her son asked a question of her.

The scent of sage filled the small room with promise. One after another, several families had lived in this room and baptized it with their odors, their greases, sicknesses and deaths. The odors lingered after the families departed. She was happy with the sage that now cleansed her nostrils, willing to risk discovery of the pagan ritual.

Soon her trial would be over and Domingo would be at her side. He worked full days in the burning sun, forming adobe tiles and bricks. On each, he marked a small "x," his own mark before the clay dried. Many others worked with him so that in the summer season several thousand "x" tiles piled up in the courtyard. He used some of his handiwork to build tight adobe rooms like the one Padre had given them to use.

Once the baby comes, I will scrub this room, she vowed. *With wild soap and lime it will be made new again, just as the ones Domingo builds now.*

A new cramp gripped her and she allowed her thoughts to flow into her calm place. Mercifully, she drifted into darkness.

When she awoke, the weight of the storm had broken. Outside, a clay tile torn loose in the wind dropped onto the ground—most likely a weak tile made by one of the others; her husband's tiles were strong as the oak limbs they were formed on. As strong as God, whose will must be obeyed.

Moments later she felt pressure building between her legs and raised her head, her body rigid. The pain was increasing, and with it the pressure to push. At her keening sob, one of the neophyte women rushed in. She bent and saw the dark place where the baby pressed. She turned toward the door and called, "Ayeeee. It is time."

Señora Marcia, the wife of one of the soldiers, slipped into the room, her crisp black skirt crackling against the quick tap-taps of her leather shoes. A neophyte woman followed carrying a cooking basket of steaming water with a hot rock inside, which her practiced hands swirled to keep the red-hot rock from burning through the basket.

Yes, it was time. She felt the child slipping from inside her. In her dream, white mist covered the canyon, a bright and swirling whirlpool. Her spirit wanted to enter, but the mewling made her hesitate, a sound so faint that she wasn't sure her ears could be trusted. She opened her eyes and saw hands cradling a tiny bundle. Boy or girl it didn't matter, only that she hold it before the angels came to take it to Heaven, for surely it was too tiny to live.

The baby's cry was pitiful, the bleating of a goat. She felt an ache of another kind when she heard Señora whisper, "Bring the Padre."

CHAPTER TWO

Alfonsa saw the probing look *Oxwe't* gave her. In the corner, the mother-in-law chafed in the sodden, coarse-woven skirt and shawl she had been forced to don for evening roll call. She rubbed her arms with her warn, calloused fingers, clearly anxious for the birth to be over so she could pull off the white woman's clothing and be naked once again. The old woman glared at her son until Domingo nodded his agreement to the unspoken contract between them, and, apparently satisfied, turned her back to the room and began to stir the fire.

Alfonsa remained silent, but she saw that something troubled Domingo. Even now he focused his gaze on the shoes of Señora Marcia and waited for a turn to speak. When Señora paused in her midwife duties he cleared his throat, glanced again at his mother, and seemed to gain strength from the set of the old woman's spine.

"No. We do not bring this child to the *sepxá*, the white God." His voice was bolder than Alfonsa had ever heard.

"Husband . . . we must."

"The old ways are good."

In the background his mother's voice was low and urgent. "The white God takes all we have. No more."

Outside, the rain continued in torrents. Crippled with fear that God would punish them, Alfonsa's voice was a croak.

"Please, husband. This one thing."

Señora Marcia flapped her hand as though chasing chickens

from the garden. "Willful children—don't be foolish. Of course, you will baptize your child. She belongs to God. Go!"

Domingo dipped his head in defeat, and rising, slipped from the room, his spirit absorbed by the grayness of despair. A moment later Alfonsa heard the shout of the sentry and her husband's answer, flat and uncaring. In the light of the small fire the room spun. Her friend Antonia, whose baby had joined the ancestors in the long sleep before she learned about God, collected soiled pine needles and took them away, leaving only the *tule* mat. Someone else washed her with hot water from the cooking basket, the drops sizzling on the warming rocks in the pit beneath her. The steam rose and burned her buttocks, but she did not complain.

Her mother-in-law's shadow fell across her, blocking the light of the fire so that part of her face showed grief. Wordlessly, *Oxwe't* held the baby. For a long moment she studied the tiny features, the pert nose and the tiny, dimpled chin.

"The blood will be strong," she declared.

Señora took the baby and laid it on the mother's belly. It was a girl, wizened, its skin a purple tinge the color of the sunset just after a storm. Alfonsa rubbed the tiny arms and legs with her rough fingers, wishing she had something to wrap it in.

"A cover," she whispered.

One of the women was reaching for a woolen cape when a padre rushed in. Alfonsa was glad to see it was Padre Juan Cabot, the Spanish padre who usually managed the laborers and not the spiritual matters.

He fell to his knees, his gray robe sweeping the dirt floor. He wore his stole around his neck, a sign that he was to perform a blessed sacrament in her humble house. She felt her heart swell with gratitude, even as her fingers holding the baby trembled. Uncorking his flask of holy water, he poured a few drops onto the baby's forehead and made the sign of the cross.

24

"I baptize you in the name of the Father, the Son, and the Holy Ghost." He scarcely glanced up, his attention focused on saving the baby's soul before the body ceased its breathing. "What is the name?"

Oxwe't raised her head and her nostrils flared. In the olden times a child did not receive a name for the first four years. Even then, the name was not chosen by the mother, another taboo.

Alfonsa looked for her husband, but he was not in the room. She felt her insides quake with fear, but her voice was strong.

"We call her Maria Inés."

Padre Cabot nodded. "You are a dutiful child. Now let us pray for her soul. Our Father Who art in Heaven . . ."

The others fell to their knees as Padre had taught them. Alfonsa prayed in the Salinan tongue of her Grandmother. *"Za til i, mo quixco nepe limaatnil. An zucueteyem na etsmatz; antsiejtsitia na ejtamilina an citaha natsmalog zui lac quicha nepe lima."*

The baby made a tortured, rasping sound. Alfonsa searched the room for Domingo, but he was outside, struggling, and her heart bled for him. Her husband was without regard for God's will and he did not know what was best for the child. Still, he was her husband. What was to be done? A simple thing was not simple when Padre's presence in her humble abode shook her ability to think.

The baby had been baptized and now more temporal needs must be attended to. A handful of salvia petals in the bath water would ease the baby's breathing. She eyed the tea prepared for her from the flowers and tender leaves of the chamise plant that grew along the banks of the river, but Padre was still lecturing that God would not allow unbaptized babies into Heaven. Her friend Antonia watched the floor with sad eyes.

When Padre finished he leaned close and added instruction for her alone. "My child . . . a wife must be modest in all things.

Adultery is a mortal sin, for which God's punishment is grave. You don't want to burn in hell for this sin."

Alfonsa felt her face heat with shame. Padre had seen the filthy Mexican *soldado*'s harassment of her. He knew about the rash raging on the hands of the filthy *cholo* thief, released from a Mexican prison in exchange for five years sentry at the remote outpost. The man's eyes branded her as though she were his wife and not Domingo's. For this man of the escolte, the Mission guard, and for the travelers with no women, lying with an Indian woman was a question of opportunity. No native woman had power over a white man's passions.

Padre Cabot understood this as well. His finger traced the ebony hairline of the baby and his face darkened. "I am a man of God!" His argument was with himself, for she remained silent. "I have no control over the escolte. Let God judge them for the filth they bring to my children." He picked up his crucifix and his holy water. As he turned to leave, his eyes softened into sorrow. "I will pray for your baby. And for you, my child."

Her eyes blurred. Surely he could see the baby was Domingo's.

At the door he turned back. "The soot—wash that travesty from your body. You shame God with your pagan ways. I will hear your confession before the week is out."

She nodded. From the corner of her eye, *Oxwe't* frowned.

Morning came and still the baby breathed—the chirp of a bird, but a breath for Domingo to hear as he fingered the baby's hair in the minutes before dawn. She wanted to ask if he had prayed for the child, but she took refuge in a simpler question.

"Where do you labor this day, husband? The repairs to the guardhouse are nearly finished."

He stretched his legs across the floor and she saw the calloused toes, cracked from the heat of the San Miguel sand. So much sacrifice his body made for God. If only he believed, his labors would not seem so hateful.

"The winds were mighty last night. The buildings suffer. Rain eats away two of the granary sides and one of the walls that hold the tame horses. Padre Cabot walks the grounds finding work for us." His frown dissolved as the baby took a weak grasp of his finger.

"Perhaps you will work close-by today." She said it to offer him hope, but her words did not warm his heart.

"One place the same as another."

His tone was flat, but his tongue spit out the words. She knew his heart; he missed his brother, killed in the battle at Pleyto, and his friends who had escaped back to the Tulare.

She slipped her hand through his thick black hair. "YaHa, husband. Does not God offer us hope?" She was glad when he nodded, even if grudgingly, to show he understood that the padres' God was more powerful than the gods that guided his people. Even long ago, the people had foretold the gray robes' coming. They had patiently danced the *Ku-ku-su* dance under the watchful eye of the shamans, waiting as the Old Ones foretold, for a mystical monk in a gray robe who had appeared many generations past and promised to return.

She knew the reason her husband's eyes were hard. He still had faith in Creator, the god of his tradition. He had agreed to this white God for her sake, but his body and soul longed for freedom. Now he felt trapped. It was not the escolte that kept him here—he could easily escape their snares if he wanted to. It was her—and now, the child. Without family, a man was nothing. Her prayers were the only hope he had.

When he spoke, it was his heart that formed the words, flat and hopeless. "I am like my mother. The Mission offers us a hard life."

"God brought you to me. Remember?" She traced her finger

along his back where muscle corded his taut body.

The words softened Domingo's weariness. He glanced at her fingers, rubbed raw grinding corn. Her broken skin had already left a scratch on the baby's cheek. He was silent as he rose and left the room.

Alfonsa traced the path his finger had taken along the baby's cheek. It did not matter that Domingo was *Tulareños,* the name the Spaniards gave the Yokuts; God had answered her prayers for a good man. He was half dead when she first met him, bleeding from a musket ball fired by one of the fierce-looking *soldados de cuero,* the leather jacket soldiers, the shot fired into his shoulder during the battle at Pleyto, on the San Antonio River, when some of his tribe made an attack. The cruel *soldado* Palermo, whom the neophytes called Red-eye, intended to leave him to die, but Sergeant Morales interceded and bound his wounds. When he was well enough to work, he agreed to become baptized when she explained it was the only way they could marry.

He was not happy here, but he was not unhappy. At night when the curfew time was upon them, the escolte kept a close watch. How was it a guard of five seemed to be everywhere at once? Red-eye watched him as though he might run. Domingo returned the mistrust, but his nature was proud and soon the padres placed their trust in him. He was already the straw boss for the craftsmen, trusted to build the beautiful structure.

She could hear Domingo outside, cracking a handful of nuts his strong hands had gathered from the walnut trees near the river. She would be grateful for the nourishment. She turned slightly and felt the fading heat of the rocks draw upwards through the mat to her naked skin. In her arms the baby shifted and began rooting, almost too weak to nurse. Already her heart filled with love for this tiny bird.

"This is what I call you, *t'axwe'n',* my little dove."

Her belly was dimpled where the skin had stretched as if it belonged to one of the old women. She would knead the loose skin as the women instructed. It was good that the padre allowed her two days' rest; she would lie on her mat and learn the secrets of her tiny bird.

"Come, my dove. You must drink."

Outside, the tolling bell signaled the morning hymn. From open doors in the neophyte housing and across the courtyard, voices began singing the lovely song the padres had brought from their country, the *"Cantico del Alba."* She joined her voice.

When the morning hymn ended and the baby was satisfied with its feeding, she struggled to her feet. The heating rocks felt cold and useless, but it did not matter. Her need for them was over. She would refill the trench and sweep the floor smooth so there would be room to move about. The mat she shared with her husband lay nearby, covered with the gray wool blanket she had woven before they were married. Soon it would be time to lay the baby in the cradle she had made of her burden basket, padded with a portion of dry grass she had pounded until it was soft.

All morning she held her baby and listened to the faint rattle of its tiny breath. She rubbed herbs on her nipples to ease the pain of a tiny mouth suckling. Some of the other mothers offered advice. They were kind, but the pity in their eyes created anger inside her, especially when one of them said the baby looked as small as an eaglet.

"Holy God, please let my baby live," she prayed to God who had brought rain.

Her belly was growling when Domingo entered, covered with mud from his labors, and handed her the nuts and a string of beads he had made from spiral-shaped *olivella* shells. He must have been working on the necklace for many weeks after his work was finished. Her heart swelled at the gift because she understood it was given to console her for his anger. One day she would give them to her daughter, a reminder of this day.

"Thank you, husband."

"*De nada.* It is nothing."

She accepted the gift without making mention of his speech, Spanish these days instead of his tribal tongue. Maybe the baby would settle him, but maybe not. He stood at the door watching the newest group of neophytes gather around the padre. These Tulareños were from Domingo's tribe, brought back a few weeks earlier. Some acted as though they did not want to be here.

"How are we to trust those new people from the far valley?" she asked. "They spit at us and call us lizard eaters."

Domingo smirked. "Is this a bad thing? I hate lizard."

Alfonsa made a tongue at her husband. "It is your choice. But these new people—what good can they bring us?"

His smile was gone. "More laborers for the buildings and the fields. You know this."

"More souls for Heaven, Padre Juan says."

"They will die from working in the fields and then they will go to Heaven. And their labors will go to the Spanish king."

A contraction from her after-labor took her breath away. Even Domingo stopped grouching while she kneaded the pain from her belly. Before the pain passed, the huge bell began tolling to call everyone to prayer.

"You must go, Domingo. Pray for the baby."

The strains of the Angelus filled her with awe as though the angels and the ancestors were adding their voices to the rough, untrained voices of the newest Indians. In the courtyard, Padre Martin knelt with his head down, and the strength of his prayer filled her. She joined her prayers with the others. When the hymn ended the people stood and began moving toward the church.

Surely their song pleased God. Within minutes the clouds

began blowing off toward the far mountains in the east and the sky opened to show patches of cobalt. A rainbow arched over the canyon, God's promise that there would be no more floods like the great waters the ancestors told about. So many things the padres taught were known to the Old Ones. It was as though the knowledge had been in the People from the beginning of time.

The morning passed with the sounds of laughter and hammering, chickens scratching for grain, ewes baaing in far pastures. The wagon track was too slippery for the wagons to pass so the people stayed close. Still, there was work to be done—repairing adobe tiles damaged by the rain, cleaning storm debris from the fields. When the workers returned at the end of the day it seemed as though only Alfonsa had been untouched by the clinging adobe clay. Alfonsa watched from the doorway as Padre Cabot limped toward the church, his sandals splashing through puddles, his back bent like the crook of a tree. The heavy doors opened for evening catechism. The line of weary workers, each with knees stained from kneeling in the mud, stretched into the courtyard, the padre the most worn looking of all. He had washed the grit of the field off himself, but his ruddy complexion told the story of his hard life.

An Indian woman approached him and shyly opened the blanket she had finished weaving to ask for a blessing. Alfonsa's own blanket had been blessed in the same manner, a blanket spun and woven on one of the huge looms in the weaving room when she was a girl living in the *monjério*. Tomorrow she would spread hers on the adobe tiles during Mass but for this day it would provide a warming blanket for the baby.

The last of the neophytes disappeared inside the church and the courtyard was vacant except for the sheep herded into the inner courtyard for protection against the night. Moments earlier the air was alive with the sounds of hammering, laughing children, mothers calling to each other, foremen shouting to their workers. Now only silence and the bleating of lambs. Even her husband's mother had gone to prayer.

Never had she remained behind when the others were inside the church. She shivered at the strangeness, but in her heart she felt a stab of pride. Today was the most important day of her life—except for her baptism. She had prayed for a safe birth and her prayer had been answered. Now her belly growled. Maybe the lesson tonight would be short and Domingo would return with a bowl of food for her. She smelled the cooking pots in the courtyard where the huge cast-iron kettles sat under the portico. With nothing else to think about, the smells of hominy drove her almost to madness. The *pozole* served at noontime was not enough, even though the aroma of meat made her mouth water and pains of hunger ate her from inside.

She was glad when the church doors opened and Padre Martin led his people to their supper. Domingo joined the line at the two large boilers filled with simmering *atole*. A server filled a basket with enough for the three of them while Padre watched closely to see that everyone received equal. The roasted corn soup was a favorite of hers. Domingo's as well, and many others. It was unfortunate the soup did not provide enough strength, for it was the same meal each sunrise and sunset.

How long had it been since she had taken a drink of water? The worn abalone shell lay near the door. She reached for it and satisfied her thirst with rainwater.

Something was caught in her ragged fingernail, a broken piece of corn. She bit hard on the kernel and tasted the juices inside her mouth. With so much to be thankful for, how could she think of hunger? But she could not remember a time when she did not. She had prayed that Padre's calendar might soon provide a holy day so the workers could be allowed to barbecue some cattle—fat so her body might make milk for her baby.

And now, tomorrow, a fiesta. God had answered her prayers.

Soon Domingo returned with three portions of gruel. His mother reached for hers without showing much interest; it was the polite way. She spoke to her son in Tulareños, but her tone left no misunderstanding. The white man's God was more powerful than theirs. This God was not to be disobeyed, but the men God sent to raid her tribal villages were not all of them good men, and now they held her tribesmen against their wills.

As the sun slipped behind the small mountain range that the Spaniards named for Santa Lucia, Alfonsa heard the evening roll call. After many minutes she heard her husband's name called. At the sound of her own she struggled to her feet and crept to the door, but exhaustion had stolen her voice and the words came out as a croak. Before the escolte would think she had run away, she cleared her throat and answered in a stronger voice.

Padre Cabot acknowledged her with a smile and leaned to speak to the name taker. She relaxed; Padre Cabot would make it all right. Padre Juan Martin was strict, but Padre Juan Cabot wore kindness on his cloak.

CHAPTER THREE

At the baby's second sunrise the ringing of the bells brought Alfonsa from a night filled with confusing dreams. The baby had taken little milk; she lay barely moving in the crook of her mother's arm. Today was a special Mass to be celebrated for the feast of Our Lady of Guadalupe. Alfonsa would ask God to allow her dove to live.

A few minutes longer she tarried in bed. Outside, the creak of the *carretas,* the two-wheel oxcarts, indicated the arrival of the Ortega family—she knew without looking because each cart sang its own song on the sandy track. Soon the high-pitched squeal of white oak axles in need of tallow greasing would signal the Chaboya family's arrival from the east. A dull drum accompanied by a dozen mounted *caballeros* accompanied Señora Bonilla with her twelve children, her tight-drawn hair, and her proud airs.

Padre Martin would have no time for his people today, only for the visitors with their offerings of wine and precious news from the north.

The pealing of bells signaled the hour for Mass. Alfonsa carried her cradle into the dim church where candlelight cast shadows on the whitewashed walls. She spread her wool blanket on the cobblestone floor, in a pocket along the left wall, the women's side. Near the back to leave room near the altar for the Spanish ladies and their daughters. Two dozen neophyte children sat solemnly at the rear where they could squirm when the service grew tiresome. Some of the boys who had mastered their letters were scratching their names on the walls with twigs. As he passed, Padre Martin smiled at their industriousness. For all his rules, he was patient with the children.

The sermon ran long this morning, in Spanish for the visitors who traveled from their faraway haciendas to celebrate this important holy day. But a portion was spoken in the language of the People. Padre Martin had worked hard to learn the language his fellow padres called Salinan. When he faltered, he continued in Spanish.

The neophytes were required to learn this language and although some, like Domingo, resisted, the Spanish language brought many words to express the tools and the ideas the padres brought to the people. Alfonsa loved the lilting sounds. Today she leaned close to hear every word.

Domingo was learning Latin and she was of little help; the language was confusing beyond the prayers and songs she had committed to memory. He stood in the balcony at the back of the church with the other musicians and singers and she heard his voice when the neophytes began a new hymn accompanied by a violin, bass viol, flute, trumpet, and drums. Some younger boys played reed, rattles, whistles, and shakers, but they stood to the side where they would not disturb.

When Domingo first joined the others, it did not seem possible for such ordinary men to create these sounds—each member a field laborer like himself. Alfonsa had never heard the angels sing, but she imagined them in these voices.

During the "Alabado," the thanksgiving song, the children's voices began, high-pitched and pure, and the people followed. The words came easily, for they sang this hymn often throughout the day: "Lift your hearts in joy and exalt Him, in the Blessed Sacrament all Holy, where He the Lord, His glory veiling, comforts souls true and lowly."

Always, her tears formed at the beauty of the words. At the beauty of the chapel as well. Padre had asked his childhood friend Munras, who was now a renowned painter in Monterey, to make an extended visit of many months in order to oversee the painting of the church. Surely, once Señor Munras and his workers finished, the church would be more beautiful than Heaven itself.

Señor Munras directed his workers to paint an *ojo de Dios* high over the altar so that the "eye of God" would watch over everyone in colors so vibrant that the pupil caught the glow from the candles. On this fiesta day, the painters had not completed the cloud surrounding it, but already golden rays of sunlight seemed suspended from the wall as if floating by themselves. The neophyte boys who served as altar boys tried to avoid stepping on the left side of the altar, where graves were set beneath the tiles holding the remains of beloved padres who had served the church well.

When she could no longer endure the scrutiny of the "eye," Alfonsa lowered her gaze to her favorite statue, that of *Nuestra Señora*, Our Lady, and, on the other side of the altar, San Jose, always smiling and welcoming. Under the painted eye stood a statue of a fierce-looking San Miguel holding a scale. Padre used the statue when he spoke about the Day of Judgment, when the sins of a poor Indian would be remembered. When her trepidation grew too great to bear, she turned to study the other two statues, San Francisco with his birds and his soft eyes, and on the other side, San Antonio holding baby Jesus. These were not so fearful.

Today, as with each time she entered, the church had a new look. Señor Munras had spent the week directing the neophytes in painting soft pink Castilian roses and pomegranates on the whitewashed walls with eagle feather brushes, a slow and tedious job. Each morning she paused in her work to watch the painters transform the church into a place where God seemed to be among even the lowliest neophyte. The first church had been built by her father and the others, but it burned to the ground when she was a girl. This one was partially built by Domingo, from bricks so vast in number that workers had been building bricks before he arrived. It took three years until they lined the hard sand for as far as the eye could see, baking to the consistency of stone. This one had curved, oven-baked tiles for the roof instead of *tule* thatch, so rain would not melt the mud walls and fire could not devour it.

The huge overhead beams drew her gaze upward. Each time padre's sermon went long and her belly rumbled with hunger, she thought about the day the beams arrived in a caravan of carretas that rolled into the courtyard just as the evening bells were tolling. At first the people had been too shocked to speak, but slowly the talk grew and she ran with the other unmarried girls to where the heaving oxen rested patiently. She stroked the massive wood beams and tried to imagine a forest of such majesty. Her father and some of the others had hewn the beams from pine trees that must have brushed the sky before they were cut down. Afterwards the neophytes and the padres carted them over a hand-cut trail from San Simeon. Surely God was happy with His house, and with the people who created it.

She saw the high green rostrum on the side of the church where Padre Martin climbed to read God's word with such authority that no one moved. The sounds of children scratching on the walls, the coughing and the rustling of the clean Sunday tunics and petticoats of the Spanish families standing at the front—even the bleating of the sheep outside—ceased while the word of God was read.

Today, Padre Martin wore a forest green quilted chasuble over his flowing white robe, his sleeves so wide that his hands were hidden when he stood at the altar with his back to the people. His singsong voice was muffled by the vastness of the long room.

She closed her eyes, pretending to tend her baby but really catching a quick nap while the padre droned on. Her baby made tiny sleep sounds in the sling across her breast and other mothers honored her with approving looks. She bowed her head and prayed, "Holy Madre, help the angels keep my *a p'xa* safe."

God was not in the church this morning for her. Maybe for the brightly dressed high-born Spanish women with their hair caught in their high combs and black veils that shrouded their light faces with mystery. Many of them only attended Mass on Sundays and holy days when they made the long trek from their ranchos to the Mission. For them, church was a privilege. But her thoughts were not on the service today and her knees ached from kneeling. In her mind she walked to the river and stood in the languid water, catching salmon with her bare hands for their supper. At the offertory, a few silver coins jingled in the collection basket, gifts from the regal families who feared hell's gates.

An hour later the service ended. Alfonsa scrambled to her feet and joined the line of people who followed Padre Martin outside for the morning meal.

She watched the young unmarried girls and bachelor men make their way to the refectory to eat together, the opportunity to gaze at each other as valued as the food they received. A good thing they did not expect more than a small bowl of porridge because the previous year's harvest had been short. Much of the grain had been sold or traded, and what remained had to be divided among many. She and the other married women were sometimes given a ration of beans, wheat, and corn, and an occasional piece of meat when a horse or cattle or mutton was slaughtered. She always gave her husband the larger portion because he worked hard, but hunger rode inside her belly, as well. Her own portion was never enough, and soon the child would require some of her share, as well.

Padre Cabot took his place beside the cast-iron kettle, watching to see that no one received more than the others. Alfonsa hid her pride when his frown lifted at the sight of his newest convert. "My child, all is well?" His eyes were soft for the tiny head barely seen beneath the rabbit skin cushioning the cradle. "Soon we must teach the child to speak in order that we have a new voice to praise the Lord."

Domingo hung his head without expression as the padre laid a blessing on the baby's forehead. Alfonsa dared a quick glance, but her husband turned away. He looked so weary. For a young man his back was already bowed from the weight of his labor. He had been working since he recovered from his wound, two years earlier, and his strength had never fully returned.

The *Playaños* who lived on the other side of the mountains where the ocean breezes cooled the land claimed the sun was hotter here than anywhere else on earth. Alfonsa did not know about this for she had never traveled over the mountains to the blue waters. Her grandfather had traveled there. Domingo, too, many times with the escolte, when the soldiers escorted a vast train of slow-moving carretas drawn by the gentle, patient Mission oxen. The trips were made in secret, the hides dropped off the side of the cliff onto the beach for *Yanqui* smugglers to collect. Domingo carried back small olivella shells for her, a string of beads she now wore around her neck. At one time, before the padres came, she would have been a wealthy woman with such beads, but the padres had brought bright-colored glass beads, and seashells were no longer used as money.

In her small room, her portion of porridge made her mouth water. She scooped a finger's full, and another, and another, swallowing without tasting until the basket was empty. Padre Martin saved the thicker mush at the bottom for the children who memorized their catechism. It should be saved for the men, but Padre did not concern himself with such earthly matters.

In the afternoon she would walk to the river and glean walnuts and pine nuts. She would not take all. She would share them with the tree squirrels so all might survive the coming winter.

Sunday was always a day of rest, but today was even more special—a feast day. All week they had been working hard to prepare food for the guests. Already, music and laughter came from the courtyard where the lovely *señoritas* in full-skirted dresses with many petticoats flitted their fans at the handsome men in their high-heeled boots and thin leather trousers decorated with conchos, round hammered discs of silver, to show their wealth. Padre Cabot had ordered cattle and sheep slaughtered. Today the neophytes would fill their bellies with meat. Domingo was outside with the other men, playing *peu*. Her heart lifted at the sound of his laughter. It was good, hearing them play their games, calling out wagers as they bet against each other. As she watched her husband's team trying to find the eagle's bone the opposing side had hidden, she smiled. He was very good at this game. His team would win the counters.

Padre Cabot was in serious discussion with his brother, a tall and distinguished priest who had ridden down from Mission San Antonio on an excellent horse, his riding skills as natural as the finest caballero. Alongside Padre Pedro, Padre Juan looked like a sailor—or a common fisherman as his nickname indicated: *"El Marinero."* So different, the two brothers, but their regard for each other was obvious. Alfonsa watched the two talking with their heads together. They spoke in low voices that carried to her ears only.

Padre Pedro gestured a long finger skyward with each point he made. "Our ranchos do not assure enough grain to feed the neophytes and guards during the years of drought. We are establishing another ranch at San Benito. The horses and cattle increase faster than the grasses. Some of the younger mares we are sending to the seashore."

Padre Juan nodded, his eyes filled with concern. "There are many who cast an envious eye on our lands. It seems they are waiting to petition the Mexican government. Should New Spain prevail in its war against our Spanish homeland, I fear the Church may suffer."

His brother nodded his agreement. "All we have worked for—the neophytes have worked for—could be lost. We must pray fervently this doesn't happen. Spain must retain her hold, however inattentive she may be to us."

The two walked on, still talking, but Alfonsa was not concerned about the future. Two such powerful men could stop any danger. Even one padre, alone.

Domingo ran over from the field and sat down at her side, winded and sweating.

"Your sides heave like the horses," she teased.

"Play is harder than work," he admitted.

She watched as a string of weary neophytes entered the courtyard, their eyes dark from lack of sleep. These were the vegetable growers. They filled their bowls and returned in the direction they had come.

"Look at those poor men. Sitting all day and night in a ring around the fields so that deer and possum do not eat our crops."

"They sing and clap on dark nights. They play *peu* in the full moon. Anything to make noise," Domingo said.

She smiled. "God willing you could join them. It is not so hot to work in the night."

He played with a coil of her hair. "I would miss sleeping with you. The ear of corn is not what I wish to nibble when I am hungry."

"Husband!" She looked around to see who might be listen-

41

ing, but there were only the two of them.

He grinned. "Maybe I should ask Padre. Soon it will be winter and those men will be done. Then they have time to nibble other ears."

She stuck out her tongue at him. "Go play your gambling games. Your friends deserve your wickedness."

After he sprang to his feet and returned to the game she was sorry she had spoken. If he grew tired in his game and needed to rest, next time she would take his place. It would give him a chance to watch the baby sleep. Maybe he would agree that his little dove had grown stronger during the night. Later they would walk to the place of the soothing mud. The sulphur mud that smelled of bad hens' eggs would ease Domingo's weary muscles. Hers, too, after her body healed. Until then she could soak to her thighs and keep a watch for bears.

Grandmother had shared stories of grizzlies rolling in the mud to cure their own aches and pains. In her time the willows and the *tules* were thick with bear. Many of the People wore the scars of the grizzly, but fewer showed new scars. Now that the soldados hunted the grizzly with muskets, the people could fish and hunt without worry for the bear—only for the quicksand.

When the baby became fretful, Alfonsa walked about the courtyard, careful to stay out of the way of the fast horses and the caballeros with their trick roping and fanciful stunts, danger-ous acts performed for the sake of the young girls watching. No matter what the status of their birth, young women were gig-gling behind their hands, waiting for music and dancing to begin in the square. From the monjério where the unmarried girls lived, Señora Morales's voice sailed in the wind.

"Come, come, children. Padre waits to give his blessing. Tardiness is a sin. We must be saintly in our endeavors."

Her heels clicked down the cobblestone arcade as she passed with her young girls in tow, each casting a wistful glance at the sleeping baby. The girls had reason to cast eyes. The Señora kept them busy from first light until last, when she locked their barred room with a heavy iron key and returned it to Padre Juan Cabot for safekeeping. He slept with it under his pillow. No soldado or passing traveler would gain access, although many had tried.

"Come, come. Already the little orchestra tunes its instruments in preparation. Remember, you may only dance the quadrilles. These dances have been celebrated since my grandmother was a girl. Good, decent dances that will benefit the virtue of a young lady. Perhaps a young neophyte will notice and Padre will form a marriage on your behalf."

Alfonsa smiled at the excitement of her friends. Not so many months ago she had been one of them. It was whispered that no one worked as hard as the unmarried girls, and having been one, she agreed. No small miracle when a husband was found.

One of them leaned close and whispered, "We are on our way to the Wishing Chair." Her giggle was picked up by the others, their bead necklaces bouncing off their small breasts. Each was dressed in her finest petticoat and small, woven hat.

"May God grant you a blessing," Alfonsa called in Spanish as the laughing girls hurried along the arcade.

"Gracias!" one called back before she disappeared into a doorway

Their excitement restored her energy. In her head she was one of them again. She imagined Señora Morales shushing them with her small, nervous flutters while they waited to take turns. It was a special day worthy of a reward. The children would get a small sweet cake. The maidens would get a sweet treat as well, but for them, the Wishing Chair was their favorite. Her first sight of the red velvet chair with gold fringe and hard wooden arms was like seeing the golden throne of Heaven that Padre talked about. She had waited for her turn on the chair, her heart beating so rapidly she thought she might take flight, like a hummingbird, to the top of the ceiling.

She sat in the chair on many other feast days, always with a wish for a good husband. It was not long afterward that Domingo was carried wounded into the infirmary and laid on a pallet with the others who had been injured in the battle.

Señora Marcia attempted to apply an ointment before binding his wounds, but Domingo glared at her with such dark hatred that the soldiers were fearful for the lady's safety. Corporal Rios insisted the prisoner be shackled to the wall while Padre summoned an old man who still practiced medicine in the old ways. Alfonsa was allowed to pick the herbs needed, accompanied by one of the older neophyte women. When she entered the infirmary with her hands filled, Domingo heard the slight footstep and looked up. The ancient healer chewed the herbs between his worn teeth until they were soft, and used them to pack the wound. Afterwards, he hobbled from the room and returned with fire ants he had collected on a twig. One by one he placed the ants on the swollen, inflamed tissue. When the ants had vacated the twig for the decayed flesh, the old man stuck the twig in the prisoner's mouth. Padre Martin was nearby, watching, and he saw the prisoner glance at the girl and reject the twig, preferring to withstand the pain with his own control.

Later, it was the padre who suggested the marriage between them, and both agreed.

While the young Yokut's fever raged she was allowed to sit on a hardback chair beside Domingo's pallet. Despite their language differences she tried to make him understand he would need to reject the sun spirit and the moon spirit because these no longer blessed the land with food and water. They were spirit of animal and not of man. Domingo listened without expression while she explained that he would spend eternity in hell if he did not accept the powerful white God.

Once Domingo was no longer in danger of death, she returned to the monjério to weave blankets for sale to the immigrants entering the valley. He later teased her that he fell in love out of boredom, and he was only half-teasing because he was always looking for something to occupy himself. One of the neophytes wounded in the battle against the fierce Yokuts spent hours carving a small wooden flute. When he saw Domingo watching, he offered both the lump of wood and the small knife. One of the other neophytes noticed and stood ready to attack should the pagan try to kill one of them, but Domingo did not press his advantage.

When the small flute was complete, and Domingo's wounds sufficiently healed, he stood outside the narrow, barred window of the monjério and played a song for her.

From the arcade Alfonsa watched the vaqueros turning their horses in tight circles, putting the steeds through intricate maneuvers using only the pressure of their knees. Soon they would begin the sport of *carrera de gallo* where young neophyte boys would bury a cock up to its neck in the sand and dashing caballeros would race past on their horses, trying to pluck it out at a gallop. They would place bets on the outcome, the competition a serious affair for the caballeros who wanted to show off their skills for the daughters of the ranchos.

Her thoughts returned to her baby. The tug on her breast seemed stronger; perhaps her prayers were heard. As the sun hung overhead in the crisp, clear air left by the storm, sounds of the Mission filled her with satisfaction. Music from the small group of Indian musicians salted the air with dance music as dancers formed a circle.

Padre Martin was speaking to Señora Morales. "See that your girls do not fall into temptation when they dance. No touching except of the hands."

Señora's dark eyes brimmed with sincerity. "As always, Padre. They will be virtue itself."

"See they retire before the drinking gets out of hand."

"*Sí*, Padre. They will be locked in their monjério long before dark."

He turned to chastise a couple who had arrived from one of the ranchos. "No waltzing," he called. "A godless dance for inciting lust."

Señora Morales nodded. "I have received a letter from my sister saying that the dance was brought to San Diego by an American sea captain who is very popular with the ladies."

"Señor Cooper? I have heard of him."

"My sister says he attended a dance in a private home and taught the dance. The next day he lifted anchor for Monterey. By the time he arrived, the dance was already being practiced there."

Padre frowned. "This does not surprise me. A determined caballero on a fast horse is the devil's handmaiden."

Secretly, Alfonsa wished some of the daring caballeros would break Padre's rule. The new form of dancing was exciting to watch, even if the neophytes were forbidden. But the contra dancing was exciting, too. In her heart she joined the dancers who lined up in groups of four for the dancing that would occupy them until the neophyte girls were escorted away. Neophyte boys were allowed to stay a bit longer, and the *gente de razón*, the Spanish and Mexican high-borns—until the band fell asleep at their instruments. It was ironic; now that she was married she could stay until her husband directed her to leave, but already her eyes drooped with weariness.

Some of the people hurried to finish their work so they could join the celebration. A braying burro led by a small boy passed along the quadrangle, its twin baskets filled with cactus apples hanging over the small creature's haunches almost to the ground. A dog trotted after him ignoring the flock of chickens scratching in the sand. From a rooftop a rooster crowed and opened its wings to catch the morning sun. A cart and a yoke of oxen lumbered past, piled high with ropes of garlic and chilies still wet from the field. The air smelled fresh with the new-washed scent of rosemary and wild mint from the kitchen garden to mask the stench of bat guano and nesting pigeons under the sheep-gate near the fountain.

The tang of roasting meat, squash, hot tortillas, and bread baking in the outdoor *horno* made Alfonsa's mouth water. The loaves were intended for the Spanish and Yanqui guests who were conversing with each other beneath the portico, but today Padre Cabot had promised her a slice of the fine wheat bread with honey as a reward for bringing a newly baptized soul into the Church. She would carry it to where Domingo rested and share it with him.

A dozen neophyte women sat on blankets stretched on the hot sand along the outside wall of the church, their eyes closed and heads tipped back to appreciate the sounds of chasing children and men's laughter. They sat with backs hunched, their bare feet dusty and thick-soled from a lifetime of walking. Some of the younger neophytes copied the padres' example, but she preferred to feel the sand beneath her feet. The señoras wore boots bought off a black market trading ship from Boston, but even if she were offered the finest pair by one of the gallant captains who sometimes visited the padres, her feet were already too wide. The tight leather would pinch the blood from her toes and she would have to crawl into church on her hands and knees.

A stab of pain pricked her insides, a burning that had appeared after the birth of her baby. She allowed her thoughts to float into the spirit world where Grandmother waited, and the pain passed. She studied her roughened fingers and wondered if the old women had been pretty in their youth. Soon it would be herself sitting there. Her heart heated with self-pity; one day of rest and tomorrow the work began again.

Across the courtyard Domingo approached with something hidden behind his back. She straightened and eased the worry from her face. Today was good. The courtyard was alive with singing and laughter, and men talking and playing shell games until the noontime bells.

"Rub this on your fingers. It will help." Domingo stood before her, grinning, a portion of lamb's wool greasy with lanolin in his hands.

Her heart filled with love for him. A gift for the baby, as well. She could rub herself and perhaps the baby would find it easier to nurse. Domingo seemed at peace today. Perhaps he would enjoy the feast.

"Will you dance today?" she dared to ask.

"I must take my turn playing the music."

"A poor husband you make."

Laughter bubbled at the edge of his eyes and he placed her shawl over his head like a headdress. "Come, we dance the *Kuksu'I! Tu-tu-tu—*."

She glanced quickly across the courtyard. "Stop your howling. You know Padre has banned that dance. You say this like a child to vex me."

The laughter erupted. "So you do not want to dance. Maybe I do the Bear dance. *Hau'-wa-ya, he'-ne-ye, hau'-wa-ya, he'-ne-ye. He'-ne-ye . . .*"

Like she had seen Señora Morales do, she wiggled her finger at him. "You are uglier than the coyote. Go on, get out of my house. Go eat a bear turd."

She smiled when her husband threw off the shawl and gave her cheek a light brush with his knuckle. She fingered the string of beads he had tied around her neck, shells warm against her skin, reminding her of his kindness. A good husband she had prayed for. It *was* good, this marriage.

CHAPTER FOUR

The following day, after the third morning bell called the workers to their labor, Alfonsa waited for the *majordomo* to assign the chores. The last overseer had died and this new one was puffed up with pride and not used to power. Bad enough that he was in league with the soldados so he would have an easy life, but she had chosen Domingo over this man when he wanted to marry her and now hatred burned from his eyes for both of them.

I will give you no reason to punish my husband, she vowed, but she kept her gaze on the ground so he would not make her duties harder.

Soon the sound of hammers and chisels biting into pine logs was muffled by the grunts of young neophytes carrying adobe blocks to complete the new rooms along the arcade. She struggled to keep her eyes open while weariness weighed her limbs. It had been a difficult night, but the baby had taken a bit of milk several times. She prayed the majordomo would not notice her exhaustion.

Padre Cabot's voice was kind as he pointed to a spot outside the large room where the huge looms were kept. "My child, you will sit under the portico and work with the women."

Señora Marcia approached, carrying one of the padres' frayed altar vestments. "Don't sit there. Find another spot." She waited until Alfonsa obeyed before she gave a conspiratorial whisper to the priest. "Do not concern yourself, Padre. I will see that the women work for the glorification of God." She offered a tight smile and added, "Your altar chasuble is in danger of falling apart."

"If only God were to change the King's mind and we were allowed to trade openly with the Yanquis. The foreign ships taunt us with their bounty." The padre returned the smile with a furrowed brow and sighed. "We will pray the supply ship arrives, but if it fails, we must provide for ourselves."

"The King sends one supply ship a year—if it doesn't perish in the storms on the way." Señora Marcia pursed her lips. "It is common knowledge that Padre Martinez grows wealthy with his illegal trade. The Yanqui ships are only too happy to take his hides. They allow two dollars credit for each for the luxuries they carry. Can you imagine what luxuries we could afford?"

"Even you, Señora?" Padre Cabot smiled. "Each time I travel to San Luis Obispo de Tolosa, I am tempted anew by Padre Martinez. He has made quite a reputation for himself."

She lowered her voice to a whisper. "They say he hides his gold and silver under the grain at the *Asistencia*.

The padre glanced around to see who might be listening. "Let us hope the authorities have not gained such information. It will sharpen their lust for our lands if they think we hide gold inside our ragged vestments."

Alfonsa had seen the gold men brought back from their trading on the Coast. She wasn't sure where it was kept, but it was none of her concern. There was much gold in Alta California. It was not coin that Padre lacked, but cloth—and thread to sew it.

Upon hearing such a preposterous idea from Padre's lips, Señora Marcia's humor seemed to be restored, for it seemed to Alfonsa that the woman's voice lifted an octave.

"This chasuble will be as good as new when I finish. And I will pray the supply ship arrives soon. God willing, Spain does not forget us with all the wars they are waging in Europe."

"Amen." He glanced toward a commotion occurring in the courtyard and dismissed her with a curt nod. "May God reward your labors, Señora."

Señora Marcia responded with a modest nod and turned to arrange her skirts before taking a seat on the narrow wooden bench where the padre had indicted Alfonsa to sit. The woman smoothed the frayed garment over her knees and threaded her needle of fine steel before glancing over to supervise the others. Alfonsa took a place on the brick floor with the other Indian women. *Oxwe't* was among them. The old women did not mend the padres' garments, only the foreign ladies were worthy of such an honor.

One of the neophyte women gave a wracking cough that echoed beneath the portico. Surrounded by piles of raw wool already washed and dried, Alfonsa lowered her head and began to card.

Señora Morales paused on her way to supervise the young girls who were spinning and weaving in a secure room. The two women discussed the previous day's feast; the quality of the beef roasted over the spit, the dancing and the pies and cakes created for the occasion. For the neophytes, the hominy had been cooked in lime and drained until the water ran clear, then a quantity of onions, chilies, and other vegetables were added along with fresh, roasted pork.

When Señora Morales finally left, and Señora Marcia returned to her quarters for another length of silk thread, the neophyte women whispered in their Salinan tongue about their concerns.

"The stores of ground corn have been used up for the fiesta meal."

"Some of the visitors will not return to their ranchos for many days. Where will food be found for those remaining?"

Alfonsa glanced across the courtyard to where her friend

Antonia was grinding corn on the *metate* and her insides heated with guilt. Antonia seemed to be having difficulty. Kernels of corn fell to the ground before they could be ground into meal. Her friend tried to catch them, her face dotted with beads of sweat, a deathly pallor of illness on her lovely olive skin. She looked up in confusion and struggled to stand. Alfonsa stood and started forward, but Antonia had made it to her feet and was walking away. When she disappeared around the corner, the majordomo began walking toward the arcade.

"One of you, take over. We have to eat. Who's it to be?"

Alfonsa shrank back, but it was on her that his gaze fell. The man pointed toward the corn-strewn metate and indicated with his thumb that she was to take up the chore.

As Alfonsa gathered her cradle, she heard the older women clucking under their breath. They exchanged knowing glances and frowned at her.

In the shadows, two of the escolte laughed. One said something crude to the other, and Alfonsa felt her face heat. Surely the majordomo knew the need for her purification before she could be allowed to prepare food. From the portico her mother-in-law came to her defense, shaking her head and uttering a string of words under her breath. Alfonsa glanced over to where the two Mexican soldados watched and knew it was hopeless; the Indian overseer had his own position to consider. Alfonsa could do nothing but lash her cradle to her back and begin her task.

Coarse sand bit into her knees as she crouched over the metate. Her thick mantle of hair covered her eyes, masking the corn kernels that Antonia had boiled in lime until they were soft. Her knees were already cramped and she had scarcely begun. Now she would spend the morning working the corn into meal for the soldados' tortillas.

She began rolling the *mano* and at first her anger gave her an advantage until her arms tired and she slowed. The grinding was normally assigned to the newest neophytes. Some did not mind the task, but the sameness of the chore wore on Alfonsa, body and spirit. Padre Pedro Cabot claimed that San Antonio Mission had a water-powered gristmill where many *fanegas* of corn could be ground in a day, but San Miguel had only women.

The deer-sinew straps of the cradle across her forehead flexed with each repetition. For now the baby slept, but soon the child would need changing and there was no more pounded grass to replace the soiled.

Alfonsa worked the corn beside seven other women, each pushing rounded stones over their flat slabs of rock, grinding the hulls off the soft, cooked corn. Her thoughts flew to a place of freedom until the meal was almost ready to shape into tortillas. She stopped to test the consistency, added another handful from the *tule* basket next to her, and started again. It mattered not that her back was already weary or that her breasts felt ready to burst with milk, but she worried for her baby. Weariness blinded her as she reached for another handful of corn.

Across the courtyard, Red-eye stared at her with a smoke stick hanging from his lips and the look of madness in his eyes. She ducked her head with a silent prayer that he would not harass her this time, but it was not to be. With a quick slash of his flattened hand across the air to toss away the smoke stick, he silenced his *compadre*'s words and started toward her. Too terrified to whimper, she looked for Padre, but he was elsewhere, tending to business. The corridor was scattered with other neophytes, none brave enough to lift their eyes to help.

The cruelest of the escolte, Red-eye was feared by the people. It was he who tried to have Domingo killed at the time of his wounding, the reason—it was whispered—was from the hatred that festered deep inside the Mexican soldado's skin because he was ashamed to be one of them. A generation or two back, his blood ran as deep as the people he guarded and he could not forgive them for that. His prison sentence was commuted in exchange for service at the Mission, but it was whispered that the *mal galico*, the rotting disease that scarred his body, was eating his brain. He did not care that he spread disease to the Indians. He spent his days and nights seeking a woman to lie with.

Alfonsa prayed nightly for God to remove him from the earth. Maybe he knew. Maybe this is why he pursued her in the dark corridors and at the river. Already it was too late for her; she had seen the tender lesion on her private parts. Maybe the rotting disease was already growing inside her, but, if so, she prayed that her baby be spared.

His boot tip kicked a rock toward her and she knew without looking up that he was nearly upon her. Fear made movement impossible. She felt the handful of corn drop from her numbed hand and scatter among the kernels spilled by Antonia, and she folded her chin into her chest, too scared to breathe. It was good that Domingo was elsewhere, carrying the beams to build supports for the new wine vats, too far away to hear her if she cried out. But she would not cry out.

The soldado's saber clanked against the metal buttons of his leather jacket with every step. He was searching for a reason to discipline her. She heard the spilled corn breaking under the weight of his feet and she knew he had found his reason. Wasting food was a mortal sin.

The cruel one's shadow covered the metate, so close that she could smell the rancid grease, sweat, and spilled wine on his reeking jacket. He stood silently, his fingers tapping the saber at his side. Pressing her fear down, she tried to move her fingers. If she could resume her work, perhaps he would return to his friends. But, she knew better. It mattered not that she had done nothing to bring the lash upon herself. He was bored and the other guards were watching.

His boot nudged the basket of ground corn and part of it spilled. Reaching down, he picked up a handful of sand and let it sift through his fingers into the clean corn.

"Grind it again. Finer. We don't eat like the pigs. And clean out the sand. I want my tortillas so I don't break a tooth. Understand?"

Quailing, she emptied her basket of ground meal onto the stone and started picking out bits of rock with trembling fingers. Above, the man laughed.

Padre Cabot approached from the steps of the church, his threadbare gray robe swaying in his haste. Relief flooded through her and she released the air that was burning in her lungs, but she dared only a few shallow pants lest the soldado notice. Still, it was enough to restore her as the padre stepped between her and the soldier. She looked up and saw that sweat rolled down Padre's face, and the top of his head, shaved into a monk's tonsure, was sunburned and covered with dirt.

At this moment his gritty hands were pressed together in the pious manner he used when he called upon God. But his voice warbled as he faced the soldado. "Surely this child does not make a problem. She is one of the most obedient of our neophytes."

The soldier straightened to his full height and gestured toward his musket. "Bah—you would defend the dead, Padre. She is lying. Do you deny that for these people, lying comes more naturally than the truth? No, I thought not. Bad enough we must eat this *diablo's* gruel. Last night it was like eating pebbles."

The padre's ruddy face was flushed with anger. "Yesterday's fiesta was well attended. It is not this child's fault that our stores are nearly gone. You know this as well as anyone." His voice roared until he sounded like one of the drums. "We have instructions. By the King's orders, you are not to interfere with the Church's work!"

The soldado howled like a coyote. "The King is across the ocean and we are here. You attend to your children, Padre. Leave this peon to me!"

Padre Juan was not frightened like Alfonsa. His voice grew stronger with certainty. "She will grind the corn over again. After she eats and rests."

"Hurruph!"

"The child has worked many hours this morning. She is ill."

As though by the padre's command, the eleven o'clock bells chimed, signaling to the workers that their meal and the two-hour siesta were at hand.

The soldado gave a ferocious growl. "They are all ill. Or old. Or lazy. You talk like they are your children."

"In this, at least, we agree. They are my children. Children of God."

"Well, this one is not ill. She is no longer *embarazada*. She breeds like a mare, but she no longer has the excuse. She will work through the siesta or she will wear the irons!" The soldier struck out with the tip of a worn boot and caught her in the underbelly. Lightning flashed under her eyelids and she sucked deep to keep from crying out. She edged away to protect the baby in the basket on her back.

Padre's face reddened and he reacted swiftly. "I make the decision of who will be punished. Not you!"

"Well, I say this one was deliberately fouling our tortillas. Who do you believe, Padre, one of the king's escolte—or an Indian?"

Padre Cabot wrung his hands together as though she were beyond his help. Bending far to the side to keep her baby from the soldado's view, Alfonsa gripped the mano and began rolling.

Above, the voice was oily, like the press of the olives. "*Va-monos,* Padre, go away. With all respect, surely you have other children to protect. This one is mine."

Without looking, she knew the expression in the cruel one's face. Even Padre could not be faulted if he backed off. Red-eye was in a foul mood today. His big *pistola* was missing from its holster and Alfonsa thought that perhaps he had lost a wager in the game of dice he and the others had played all morning long with some of the visitors from the ranchos.

She kept her face hidden and bore down on the stone while her mouth grew dry. But Padre had not abandoned her. He was demanding mercy.

"She must tend her child. It is the King's law—the siesta."

Something of Padre's tone infected the soldado; he growled his order to her again, but this time it lacked its former sting. "When the work bell tolls, leave the baby with the old woman and get back here. *Andale!*" Promptly.

She clamored to her feet and swept the baby to safety before he could change his mind. A few steps away she turned back to seek the padre's reassurance, but the majordomo had interrupted with a problem and his attention was diverted.

The others were lining up for their meal, a mixture of wheat, corn, peas, and beans that would give them strength for the long afternoon.

One by one the families disappeared into their rooms. She watched as Domingo's mother carried a portion to her son. Some of the escolte stretched out under the portico. The Indians spread out across the grounds, some to sleep in the cool trees at the river. She found an oak where the limbs provided shelter, took a seat, and released her baby to suckle.

Alfonsa prayed that later, when Padre Cabot passed on his way from the fields, he would convince Sergeant Barges, a sympathetic Spaniard with a neophyte wife, to do a kindness and release her for the *sepxá*'s sake. She had no care for herself, but her child was innocent. Besides, the filthy disease would devour her like it had devoured the flesh of other women. When she was gone, *Oxwe't* would rear the child, but the old woman would follow the traditional ways and she would not mention the mother's name to the child.

She had scarcely nodded off when the work bell warned her to hurry. She ran to where her husband's mother waited and thrust the cradle into her arms. Red-eye was standing in the shade, watching.

By the time she lifted the first basket of ground corn meal her arms were trembling. She willed her hands to remain steady as she waited with her eyes fixed on the ground while Red-eye made an inspection. He nodded curtly and turned away. Flies crawled over her sweat-matted hair and her scraped, bloody knuckles. Soon she finished another basket and began again.

The afternoon sun continued its path to the mountains, taking what heat remained with it. She heard *Oxwe't* clicking soothing sounds to the baby and her breasts became engorged with milk, but she bit her tongue and continued. At last the prayer bell released her from her agony.

Red-eye had moved on and the courtyard was once again a place of prayer. Without rising from her knees she joined her voice in the evening hymn. It was better, kneeling for reverence than for another's amusement. The words of the song reminded her that she should forgive her enemy. In her ear, Grandmother's words returned, spoken to the small child she once was: "What you do not want done to you, do not do to another." The voice comforted her, even if her bitterness remained.

Her burden basket was filled with corn and the weight dragged her backwards when she slipped the strap over her forehead and struggled to stand. Her mind was numb as she slowly limped through the mud into the storage area and tried to ignore the other women's curious glances. One of them helped her to slip the basket from her back. Another handed her a gourd filled with water. She drank her fill and started to follow the others to the church for evening rosary, but she had tarried too long and they had disappeared into the church. With the courtyard empty, she saw Red-eye leaning on the colonnade, waiting.

He grabbed her arm and dragged her to the common area where four others were already locked in irons. A cruel twist formed on his heavy lips and he rattled the heavy metal chains at her as if considering the idea of locking her up. She stood still, not daring to breathe lest her legs fail her. When she offered no further sport, he grabbed another man who had been brought forward for punishment and clapped the irons on that one, instead.

Across the courtyard the door to the church opened and Padre Cabot stepped out, his face as dark as the evening. Before he had advanced a dozen steps, Red-eye let out a donkey's bray of laughter, turned, and stalked back toward his quarters, the keys on his leather jacket clinking against his saber.

Padre Cabot's face seemed weary. "My child, soon I will no longer be able to protect you."

She tried to quiet the bird that was fluttering inside her breast.

He placed his hand on her arm and his other finger to his lips. "It will be announced at Mass tomorrow morning. I am being transferred to the Mission Dolores. It is God's will that I go to San Francisco. I'm sorry."

Tears blurred her vision. She wanted to take the calloused hand and hold it against her cheek, but she was afraid. Silently, she followed him into the church.

Without drawing attention to herself she found a space on the cool tiles and sank to her knees. Each recitation of the "Hail Mary" brought fresh tears that she did not allow herself to shed. Her husband was across the church, on the men's side, his eyes closed. It was no surprise that he was weary. He toiled like one of the horses, his strength replacing the men who could no longer work. Watching him stagger under the heavy loads of brick and wood made her heart ache. With so few left alive after the latest sickness, he was not hard to spot, even with the same short black hair and stooped shoulders as every other neophyte. The men were easy to tell apart, especially those whose bellies carried the scar of a hernia earned as small children carrying burdens too heavy. Some of them would be dead today but for a visiting Spaniard who showed the padres how to stitch the ruptured intestines back into the body cavity. Surely San Miguel, the saint, protected them.

She sniffed and wiped her nose with the back of her hand.

Perhaps this coming Sunday her husband's name would be on the list that Padre read off. If so, it would be his turn to go hunting or visit his relatives. He could take the days that were allowed and walk far into the forest to shoot birds with his bow and arrow. But she was not hopeful. Many months had passed since his name was called.

The rosary prayers over, Padre Martin led the congregation toward the door. She felt her tears welling again, this time for the small number of faithful that straggled out after him. Many of the men had no family left; they stayed because they had nowhere else to go. To live without purpose was to live as a slave, but they found faith in God, and that meant their souls would be saved from hell.

"Please, Grandmother, protect my daughter. Teach her what she needs to know. I am afraid."

At the steps of the church her husband's mother got in line for their meal without acknowledging Alfonsa's presence. The Tulareños were fierce warriors, the women as well. *Oxwe't* held no love for the captors of her son, but still, she remained—God had brought her to them so that she could help her son when the time came.

CHAPTER FIVE

Four years passed. With each passing summer the neophytes declined in numbers. Alfonsa fought her illness. Her people said that she was strong, or blessed, for she did not die as quickly as some of the others, even though the rotting disease remained inside her. Even her baby thrived. Instead of dying as everyone expected, the child lived, her blood strong like *Oxwe't* had predicted at the birth. As always, food was scarce but Alfonsa worked hard to see that her child had enough.

On the other side of the valley, *t'a'a'u'* devoured the hills, fire sending plumes of smoke high into the sky. Summer-fat deer raced the flames, their black tails lifted into the wind like their ears, signaling danger. The coyote and the foxes ran as well, making their way toward the river where the thick stands of willow and *tule* offered protection. No animal was hunting today. Even the rabbits ran—too panicked to cast a glance at the coyote or the rattlesnake.

Alfonsa felt the sting of a wasp on her hand and without thinking, pulled a handful of mud from the riverbank and covered her skin until the pain eased.

Vaqueros on their beautiful horses galloped into the herds, shouting and waving their hats, directing the horses and cattle toward the river. Domingo was among them, a small figure on foot, sent to fight the fire threatening the olive orchard.

Smoke entered her nostrils from the heat as it swirled around the cries of the vaqueros. Her mother had told her that in the old days fire was a welcome visitor. When it finished eating the land, it laid a blanket of ash in every direction and the rains fed it into the earth. When the long days of summer came again the earth offered fertility to the seed. Tender grass grew over the whole world and the deer grazed close to the villages, eating their fill. She closed her eyes and let her thoughts travel to the old village where Grandmother had been born. She remembered the stories Grandmother had taught her about the long-ago days.

On the day of hunting, the shaman held a great prayer ceremony. The men smoked their pipes. Each man talked to his bow and arrows with respect, asking for their help in the hunt by flying straight and true. The People celebrated whether one man or many prepared to hunt—for one man with skill and well-flying arrows could kill enough meat for all the tribe. Sometimes a hunter was so skilled that he could get two arrows into the air on the same bird, one arrow in flight while holding the second arrow in his mouth.

Alfonsa knew in her heart that Domingo had been such a hunter in the days before he came to live at the Mission. Even now he used every free hour to stalk the forest. And each time he returned with game and birds to feed his family, and even for the families of the men whose arrows fell short because they grew soft at the Mission and they had lost the skill to hunt.

One year he passed the hours of winter tanning a deer hide, leaving the horns and the head intact.

"What do you use this for?" she asked him. He smiled and said nothing, but his mother watched with eyes of pride.

"I make the deer think I am his brother," Domingo said.

On the day he hunted, she followed. When he was still in the trees, at the edge of the tall grass, he covered himself with the hide and slipped his head into the prepared skull. She watched him crawl through the grass with the skin draped around him.

When he was close he dropped to the ground, using his left hand for balance, and crept carefully with his bow and arrow in his right hand. She turned and stole softly back toward the Mission so that her scent would not give away his hiding place. He chewed tobacco to make the animal drunk when the *ts'a-kai,* blew his man-scent downwind.

Her heart had been happy as she made her way home to prepare the fire. He would return with a deer loped over his shoulder to share with the others, and even though it was not something Padre would understand, he and his mother would thank their brother deer for its sacrifice that others might eat.

For many generations the people were friends of the *t'a'a'u',* and the fire was friends with them. If the lightning did not bring the *t'a'a'u',* then the people spread out across the hills and lit the bushes with burning sticks. Each time a fire raged, the following year hunters could find game within a half day's walk. In the old days people grew fat on the meat. They used the hides for winter clothing and every part of the deer for scrapers and for tanning the leather. But since the padres' coming, the land had grown lazy. Tall bushes grew over the meadows where deer had once grown fat on grass. The cattle that the padres brought with them had multiplied until they dotted the hills, crushing the soil and terracing the land with their heavy hooves so that no new seed grew.

Today the hills were burning and Domingo would be glad.

Alfonsa led her daughter to the river. From the cool shade of the willows they watched the flames touching the far bank of the Salinas. The river was wide. The fire would not cross—but the rabbits did not know this.

She waited in the shadows until one ran close enough that she could kill it with a rock. When it finished writhing, she cut the fur at the belly and the base of each foot, and pulled the skin off. It would make a soft cape for the child when winter came, and the meat would be welcome. Her mouth watered as she pulled the entrails out. Unable to wait any longer, she tore a strip from a thigh and chewed it raw, enjoying the toughness of sinew and muscle in her teeth. She pulled off a second piece and gave it to her daughter.

"Eat, little dove. It will make you strong."

In the distance a cow was braying from pain. One of the vaqueros rode up to it and used his lasso to pull it forward. When the cow was close enough to the place where the butchering was done, he pulled his knife and slit its throat. A handful of neophytes, led by Domingo, waited until the cow ceased quivering before they began butchering it with sharp knives. The vaquero turned and rode back toward the fire line.

Domingo and the others gutted the animal with quick, practiced movements. In minutes the entrails lay in a pile. They looked around and saw that no padre or soldado was watching. With short stabs of the butchering knives they tore mounds of fat from the belly and stuffed it into their mouths.

Alfonsa watched with the taste of rabbit on her own tongue. The flavor was welcome, but the rabbit had no fat. She smiled when Domingo began cackling like a raven. Another joined in and they began flapping their arms in a raven dance while they grabbed another handful and chewed. *"Grasa!"* Fat!

She waited until Domingo ceased his dance and saw her standing nearby. He grinned and his face seemed distorted. It had been many months since any of them had looked so happy. When he handed her a bundle of fat she pinched off a portion for her child and another for herself, and let the taste fill her senses. The rest she tucked into her palm for *Oxwe't*. Her mother-in-law would be happy.

She turned to her child and murmured softly, "Come. We must go."

A hungry neophyte was striding toward them. She took her

child's hand and hurried toward the row of housing before the man could claim the meat for his own meal.

Safe again in their little room, she watched *Oxwe't* and the child stroke the skin of the rabbit they had skinned and that now roasted on the fire. The two of them responded to the secret language that she, too, had shared with her grandmother. Grandmother's spirit was here in the room, approving as *Oxwe't* whispered, "Do you remember what I taught you, little one?" The child looked around before nodding. Alfonsa watched, too. The old ways were not the ways of the padres, but the older women had to teach the grandchildren or the old ways would die. "Tell me, then."

The child began, halting between words until she grew confident. *"pek . . . xulax . . . xulep . . . xamaxus . . . pema . . ."*

"Pemaxala."

The child nodded, concentrating. *"Pek-walanai . . . xulax-walanai.* That is all I know."

"Seven makes big number, *Ta· xwe'ne'.* You can count very far."

"How many summers does *Ta· xwe'ne'* see?"

Oxwe't indicated four small stones near the doorway. *"Ta· xwe'ne'* sees *xamaxus* summers."

The child picked up the stones and placed them in her grandmother's hand, one by one. "How many summers *Oxwe't* see?"

Oxwe't considered. "Many. Before the padres come, I was."

"Ama', too?"

"Ama' was a powerful hunter. Your grandfather sleeps the long sleep before the padres come."

"He dances?"

"You know this. We talk about his dance."

The child searched in one of the small baskets where her mother's things were stored. She glanced over at her mother and Alfonsa nodded. The baskets contained valuable tools, but today was a special day. She searched among a bird bone awl used to puncture holes in the leather straps, the abalone shellfish hook that had been carried from the big waters, and a hide scraper with a broken point. The child picked out the rattlesnake's tail and returned to *Oxwe't*'s side. "Let us dance."

Alfonsa glanced at the doorway, but no one was coming. The fires on the hill required everyone to protect the crops. Everyone except the old and the very young. And those like her. Today was not a good day for her; her body was beginning to slow with the disease that was inside her. No more babies had grown inside her and this was God's punishment for her sin of lying with the soldado. Maybe tomorrow would be better.

She turned from her thoughts to listen to the sound that the child, Maria Inés, made with the rattles.

> *"hau'-wa-ya   he'-ne-ye*
> *hau'-wa-ya   he'-ne-ye*
> *   he'-ne-ye*
> *hau'-wa-ya   he'-ne-ye*

{"There's plenty,   we are glad"}

> *ta-we'—ye-he'*
> *ta-we'—ye-he'*

{"We're chewing acorns"}

> *hu'—hu'—hu'*

Her child's happiness filled her with life and hope. Alfonsa pulled off her skirt and draped it on her head, covering her hair like a coarse-woven headdress, and began the dance. Her child began clapping her hands in time as she had been taught, while *Oxwe't* watched, satisfied. For several turns they moved in rhythm to the song, the thin, childish lisp imitating her mother.

From the fire, the scent of roasting rabbit filled the room.

The three of them were Bear dancers, imitating the crouching walk and the roar of a bear dancing in the late summer when the nights were still warm and the oaks were heavy with acorns.

A shout in the courtyard brought the dance to an end. Alfonsa swept the skirt from her head and slipped it back over her hips. The child returned the rattles to the bottom of the basket for another day. Alfonsa smiled at her daughter. "*Ta ta'* will be hungry when he returns. Your father's nose will find the rabbit, and he will eat with a full heart. He will bring beef and you will help your mother make it into jerky."

Maria Inés's lips softened into a smile and Alfonsa felt her heart leap with love. "You are a fine hunter, little dove. Did you hunt like the coyote?"

"No," the child answered. "Like the bear."

Alfonsa smiled. "Would you like me to tell you the story of how Grandmother came to live at the Mission?"

"Yes," Maria Inés answered, her answer the same each time the question was asked.

Alfonsa waited beside the fire for the child to settle. Through the flames, Grandmother's image mingled with the smoke, wavered, and then disappeared as though she had been watching the dance. Alfonsa began. "Grandmother's heart was sad. She watched at the clearing when the gray robes led her people into the church. She heard the voices of the children singing words that no bird or creature in the forests had heard. She was angry, but she felt the white God's pleasure at the sounds the people made and she grew afraid. She did not want to come. The old ways were deep within her. She did not want to give up the life she shared with her husband."

"But she couldn't remain behind because she was hungry," Maria Inés said.

Alfonsa nodded. "Some of the others returned for a day or two, then for a week. One day my mother returned to gather her *topE* and to look Grandmother in the eye before she turned her feet toward the Mission."

"We have a *topE*." Maria Inés pointed to the trinket basket.

"It is the same. My mother carried it here." Alfonsa watched as her child placed it in their circle before she continued. "Soon no one was left to hunt or gather berries. Grandfather, *Ama'*, said it was not good for the people to divide."

"He was a shaman so he would know these things," Maria Inés added.

Alfonsa continued with her eyes closed. "He would not leave, and so she stayed. Soon only a few of the old ones remained. With no one to gather the seeds and no one to grind the acorns, those left suffered."

Maria Inés listened silently to the story she had heard many times.

"Grandmother's heart hungered for her family. When *Ama'* joined his ancestors in the long sleep, she gathered her *tule* mat and walked a day's travel to join her son and daughter at the Mission." Alfonsa felt her body weakening. "That is enough for this day. You finish. Tell me the words Grandmother said when she arrived."

Maria Inés nodded gravely. "It is good that my family is together again, but a sad day, too."

Chapter Six

In the summer of 1828, clanging bells broke the silence of the valley at an hour when no service was to be held. No smoke lifted from the cookhouse or the livery so the church wasn't on fire. No enemy menaced from the river or from the barren hills to the east. Every neophyte within hearing began running toward the plaza from as far as the vineyard, three leagues distant.

Caballeros from the nearby hacienda were sharing their news with Padre Martin. The supply ship had arrived in Monterey with news a year old—Mexico was expanding its independence from Spain. Changes were coming to Alta California. The whooping caballeros reined their horses in the crowded courtyard, narrowly missing Alfonsa as she tried to find safety beneath the portico. One of them explained that everyone, even the padres, would be required to sign a document swearing their loyalty to their new country.

Padre Martin hung his head for a moment before promising to sign the oath required of him, but the caballeros obviously expected something more. With a sigh, Padre had ordered the bells to be rung in celebration. The men shot their muskets into the air, startling the swallows from their nests.

By nightfall the men were drunk with Padre Martin's wine. Alfonsa waited until the room emptied before she slipped in to tidy up. She had no concern for herself—in the past fortnight her face had begun showing the ravages of disease and the men would look elsewhere for their needs. Her suffering seemed nothing when she saw Padre Martin shuffle out into the night, on his way to his quarters. His shoulders bent in worry for his people. She worried, as well, but her concern was for Domingo, for the signs of the mal galico that ravaged his body with blisters on his dark skin and baldness where his hair had fallen out. He had grown too weak to pound the nails that were forged in the blacksmith's shop; the job had been given to one of the other neophytes. Instead of overseeing the new vats where the wine would be made, the majordomo instructed him to make himself available at the farm. The grain needed planting. He could do scarcely half a day's work, but he had risen that morning to try.

"I bring this upon you," she whispered when he staggered into the room at the end of the day. "This is my sin."

Her husband waved his hand to silence her. "It is the work of the devil. Isn't that what your Padre says?" He rose up on an elbow from the mat where he had dropped. "A diablo that stalks the earth while we wait for death."

"God will welcome us when our time comes," she whispered as she held the abalone shell to his lips. She hoped the words would cool his pain as effectively as the yarrow salve she had prepared for his blisters. She had searched the river for the yellow plant and now many leaves and roots hung from the loft beam, enough to last them a few weeks. She had also boiled manzanita berries in water. The elders used it for poison oak; maybe it would work on their blisters, as well. She handed him a bit of willow to ease his pain and he began to chew, even though his gums were inflamed and his teeth loose.

It was good that she and Domingo talked of forgiveness. Padre Cabot had returned from the Mission Dolores at San Francisco and he heard her confession.

"I am happy that you have returned, Padre. The people suffer hard times."

"This life is not intended for happiness. That is reserved for Heaven."

"I will die soon."

"If God wills," Padre Cabot said. His face was hidden behind the screen, but she heard faith in his voice.

"Will the soldado go to hell?"

His voice sounded strong and sure. "That is for God to decide."

She wished she could be as sure. For her people, evil spirits had always been on the land. Some of the old Indians in the early days were still *hechiceros,* and these wizards knew the devil. Once, some of the neophytes were working on Santa Lucia peak, cutting the *pinos.* As they sought the pine trees that were big enough to be used for rafters, one of them saw a lizard lying on top of a rock in the sun. As the man looked, the lizard took its front leg and put it up at the back of its neck and took a piece of bloody skin that was growing there, and threw it at the Indian. It hit him in the head and the man fell over with a serious sickness. The others brought the man back. The hechiceros sang songs mentioning Santa Lucia peak, and their songs succeeded in fixing the man up so that he didn't die. After he recovered, a padre went out and blessed the peak in the name of Santa Lucia, and the devil no longer lived on the peak.

"Must I pray for Red-eye?"

"More than for the others, my child. His time is soon when he must meet God. He has much to answer for. Let our hearts not be filled with hatred for him. He has suffered, too."

She searched her conscience for her sins, but she could think of nothing she had done since the week before. In the front of the church she heard the neophyte choirmaster teaching the children the words of a song in Latin. The neophyte was impatient today. He rapped his stick on the music stand and his anger punctured the air. Outside, a pigeon flew from its shelter near the doorway. The music began again and the bird flew off with a twig in its beak.

In the small, dark confessional Padre Cabot gave her a penance and made a sign of the cross over her. She rose and made her way into the church where her daughter waited. Without thinking, she sank to her knees and began to pray.

It was time. Her daughter Maria Inés had reached her ten summers. Time for her to enter the monjério so that Señora Morales could train her to be a good wife. It was a tradition that she hated above any other. Her daughter would be ripped from her at an age when Maria Inés should be learning the old stories and teachings, but instead she would forget the old ways and became a stranger to her parents.

In the distance she heard the tapping of Señora's small steps approaching. Alfonsa closed her eyes and made herself still and small. She wanted to call her daughter to her side, to grip her hand and tell her that her blood was strong, but she remained as silent as a fawn and kept her disease-ravaged hands covered with a swatch of wool to prevent the disease from spreading.

Señora Morales stood in the doorway, so straight and stern in her high-neck blouse and full skirts that she seemed like a pine tree against the sunlight. Her eyes lit on the girl and she spoke without looking at the mother. "It is time."

Alfonsa felt nothing, not heat, not cold, not fear. As though she were watching the singers in the church, she motioned to her daughter. *"T'axwe'n'* . . ." To say more was not possible. The dove was Padre's daughter now.

The Señora nodded and turned without looking back to see that the girl followed. No one would dare defy the order. Her footfall on the bricks sounded like drumbeats compared to the silence of the girl's bare feet following.

Alfonsa turned to the all-seeing eye of God over the altar and bowed her head. There was no prayer in her heart so she remained silent.

She was tired. Her body hurt and she was ready to go to the bright cave, for that was how she imagined Heaven would be. When she stood, her legs barely supported her. The walk back to her house was difficult. Her eyes were nearly blind, but familiarity led her across the swept, hard-packed sand and into her room. Her back burned from blisters. But a small miracle that her body no longer required food or drink—or sleep. Still, every hour torture. She had no wish to be a saint as Padre Cabot was, to suffer for God's sake. Her prayers were for death.

Her friend Antonia entered, her step hesitant as though she, too, understood the time was near. "I will look after your daughter. She will be my blood."

Alfonsa nodded. The People would see to her child just as they had for all the other children left without a parent.

Outside, Red-eye's voice crackled with anger, the voice very close to her own door. Alfonsa opened her eyes in dread and heard the cruel one shout, "What are you hiding, there? Let me see!"

Her husband's voice, so weak, answered. "Only a small gourd of wine. My wife is too weak to eat." He sounded trapped.

The Spaniard's voice commanded the air like the thunder. "Give it over, you thief!" A moment later the gourd hit the dirt and the Spanish thunder roared once again. "*Cacique*—ten lashes for this peon."

Alfonsa dragged herself up, her wracked body barely able to make the long steps across the courtyard to the *calabozo* where all the lashings occurred. Her husband's mother was ahead, her small copper back arched in anger. A neophyte tied Domingo's hands to a post driven into the sand for the purpose of public punishments—so tightly that the ropes bit into his blistered skin. She wanted to call to him: *Please husband, plead to God to forgive your sin. The lashes will be lighter.* But she remained silent.

It was in her husband's heart alone, the choice he would make.

The Indian cacique in charge of overseeing punishment was quick to carry out the order, but Domingo would not blame the Indian.

She hid in the shadows where Domingo would not see; her husband had nothing left but his pride and he would be ashamed if he saw her. She knew her husband's thoughts without hearing them. To bring the lash on a man was worse than to treat him as a child. Perhaps, in truth, he had taken the wine for himself, not for her—inviting a quick death for himself. He was a Yokut from the Tulare, a fierce hunter and protector of his people, a man who had waged war on the Missions. Now, his job was to plant the soil with body bent to the earth, the hot sun burning his back. He did not want to live either, but the choice had been taken from him.

One by one, the lashes opened his skin.

Her tears stung as she watched Domingo use anger to belie the pain. "Is this the lash of a weakling?" He struggled to stand upright as he jeered the cacique, "End it! In God's name, end it!"

His pain singed through her and she slipped to her knees. *In God's name!* Her husband had used the words. Her tears grew thick behind her eyes where no one would see. A long time she had prayed for these words to be said. Now she knew his time was near.

"In God's name, what is this?"

A commotion in the guardhouse interrupted Padre Cabot's supper, his mutton cooling, his limbs weary from his ride to the Asistencia at Santa Margarita to say Mass for the neophytes who were harvesting the wheat. The lashings were the bane of his existence, but order could not be maintained without them. He had memorized the King's pronouncement on maintaining order among the Indians so that he might not have to take personal responsibility for a thing he hated. All he could do was to ensure that the lashings were done in the manner prescribed, publicly, at the end of the day when others could learn by example. The King's orders directed women neophytes to be punished inside the guard cell where their cries would not arouse passion in the males and risk general rebellion, and in this he concurred, but their punishment was normally endured in silence.

Some padres were known to favor the lashings—even to the point of using chains—those whose nervous constitutions were strained by their constant and mind-numbing battle to curb the vices of the people they were charged with training. Padre Cabot included these men in his nightly prayers, the fallen priests dead to all but brute force. Several had been recalled to Mexico City for this reason. One was now teaching in an academy where, hopefully, his mind could heal.

Padre Cabot pulled his monk's hood over his head in an unconscious act of contrition. When he arrived, Domingo, the carpenter neophyte with the daughter newly under Señora Morales's care, stood defiant, his eyes glazed in unnatural brightness. Blood dripped from his wounds, but Domingo seemed exalted. The light in his eyes concerned the priest. The punishment had gone too far. The instructions from his superiors were severe, but it had always been his intention to temper them with mildness and charity so as to never break the spirit, only to firmly remind the children that God watched their every transgression.

Private Palermo had arranged this. Padre Cabot watched the man's red eyes and made a holy vow. When the reinforcements from the presidio at Monterey arrived, he would see the man relieved. Until then, the escolte was scarcely able to function without him.

Two Indian women watched nearby, one standing, the other collapsed on the ground, little more than a corpse, herself. He recognized Maria Alfonsa, a penitent in the advanced stages of the illness that ravaged his Mission and that of his brother's in San Antonio. One to whom he had anointed the sacrament of the dying.

Every padre had the same complaint; each prayed fervently that the replacement soldiers might arrive accompanied by a wife and family to occupy them in this lonesome and monotonous outpost. The single men had too much time and carnality to prove good examples. Worse, many of the recruits brought with them the late stages of the mal galico from the brothels and the prisons of Mexico City.

He was worn out from petty arguments with such men. His responsibility was limited to saving the spiritual souls of the native population; harmony with the authorities was a hard-earned grace at the expense of many prayers.

The tableau before him mocked in him a sense of irony—a decent young man with good heart and soul being scourged at the pillar. Pontius Pilate must have felt the same. A soldier of the guard watched; all that was lacking seemed to be a crown of thorns. He felt a chill run through his spine. "What goes here, Private?"

"Punishment for theft."

What could any Indian want that wasn't his already? "What was taken?"

"A measure of wine."

He hesitated. Wine was a bad thing for the neophytes. Five guards against six hundred Indians required severe methods for the good of their souls. He straightened and allowed his face to harden as he had learned to do during five thousand such days. His voice was tight, but his words firm. "*Esta ley todavía está en vigor.* Finish the sentence."

The Indian in charge of the punishment hesitated. With three strokes left to go, the injured man slumped against the post without moving. Blood oozed from a dozen places. Seeing the futility of further action, the cacique let the whip fall from his fingers until Red-eye shoved the man aside and picked up the whip. The last three lashes landed with terrible force.

Alfonsa watched without flinching. Domingo's words, a challenge, already raced through the courtyard in the murmurs of the others. They had learned many things in the years they had lived among the padres. They had seen good men and bad hide behind the cloak of God. Tonight good and bad did not matter as much as mercy. Why is this so, the people would ask the padre tomorrow. Life is a preparation for Heaven, Padre would answer.

She did not think God's presence would be found in the guardhouse. The scars of Red-eye's lashes laced the backs of most of the neophytes, his cruelty the weight of his madness. Padre taught them to consider the sinner, not the sin—a week of bread and water or a few light lashes as a reminder enough in nearly all cases. But the escolte used much force as if the act of punishment brought them pleasure. The soldados spent their days complaining about their duties—serving their government in this place they called Alta California. Their assigned duties consisted of standing watch, not in manual labor, but some of them managed even these lightest of duties in ways that brought shame to the others. Theirs were not the ways that Padre taught—his rules left little that was not considered a sin—his neophytes punished as children, and yet these men performed cruelties with no fear of consequence. Surely God must weep if all men acted in such a way.

Not all of the escolte were the same. Some of them, like Corporal Petronilla Rios, wore bright smiles for the children, and even made game balls out of leather or feathers. Some had honorably taken wives from among the people and created families of their own.

Among his people Red-eye was not admired for his character. It was said that, given the choice of dying in prison or serving the King, he chose the Missions so that he might live—and yet he brought living death in his shadow.

A strange thought entered Alfonsa's head, something Domingo confessed to her in the night, from the time when she was carrying her baby.

"This week, I see the *soldado* harassing you and I want to kill him. A bad omen. A man who will soon have a new baby should not show anger." He spoke with his eyes focused on the ground so that his bad energy would return to the spirits. The *soldado* had seen him, as well. His punishment, to be locked in irons until sunrise, was nothing, but he wanted to kill the guard. The temptation had been great. Instead, Red-eye still lived and it was her husband dying.

But, first—herself.

With her remaining strength, Maria Alfonsa slowly unwrapped the woolen strips that hid her malady. Watching her husband's bloodied, still form, she felt peace descend over her as she folded into darkness and felt her spirit going to meet her husband. Her heart was his. Heaven or hell, they would be together. With a quiet sigh, her soul released.

Domingo woke from his blackness and found himself looking into the soft, loving eyes of his mother. Too weak to walk, he allowed two neophytes who were his friends to carry him. Another carried his wife and he was glad that her pain was ended. His mother began walking with purpose. He saw that his wife had fallen into the long sleep and he was glad for her.

He feared that his mother was leading them to the infirmary until she diverted her steps in the direction of a huge oak tree near where the river flowed softly north. This is good, he thought to himself. His mother does not allow him to die on a pallet, struggling to see the sky. He would not die inside a room. His Indian heart was strong, even as life flowed from his body.

Oxwe't washed the blood from her son's body, and from his wife's. She clothed her son in his fine cape, and in a loincloth made from the skin of a buck slain by his own hand. The wife she dressed in the woven *tule* skirt and cape of her people. She singed their hair with a firebrand, and sang an ancient song as she inhaled the smells that cloyed to their bodies. When the last vestiges of dishonor were purged from their skin, she pulled forth a long, sharpened piece of flint and plunged it into her heart so that she could travel to where her two sons waited.

The ancient gods would understand. It was finished.

Padre Cabot held a service for Domingo and his wife in the cemetery where many other neophytes were buried. *Oxwe't* was buried outside the walls, in the unconsecrated ground where the cactus bloomed in the summer.

CHAPTER SEVEN

In the monjério, a mosquito buzzed around Maria Inés's head. She felt the tickle on her cheek when it landed, and stilling her breath, she welcomed the slight prick. When it flew off she took a small breath without opening her eyes and waited for the moon to show itself in the airless room that imprisoned her. The small, barred window covered with scraped sheepskin prevented purifying air from reaching the forty girls that slept inside. Nearby, her friend Esperanza slept unmindful of the heat for she had found a scrap of cloth and had soaked it in cool water and laid it on her face, for she was clever. Often Maria Inés wished she could be more like her friend.

The other girls reclined on their mats, uncomplaining, but she would never get used to the closeness. Outside, a horned owl called from the tall oak that shaded the room from the moon while Maria Inés fought the feeling of suffocation. Little wonder that the elders preferred their huts. Many claimed that sickness lived in these rooms and fresh air kept them safe.

Señora Morales had fastened the door. Each night the twist of the heavy key in the lock brought with it the feeling of terror—and a longing to see her mother. Instead, the heavy wooden door clanked shut, Señora's heels clicked away, and the room was silent.

Each night she traveled in her head to the willows near the river where Brother Fox stalked the rabbits who gave their lives so their brothers might live. The call of a dove carried into the room and she thanked it for remembering her. When one of the girls sighed and turned on her mat, Maria Inés froze with fear that the girl would begin whispering. Only by being silent could she hear the sounds of the night.

Suddenly she felt a presence. In the darkness an old woman stood over her with eyes that spoke of great sorrow, her white hair seared in mourning. The woman did not speak because she was not of the living, but Maria Inés knew. It was Grandmother.

She shook her head, trying to clear the vision, but the image beckoned her to rise. Frightened, she bit back her whimper as, inside her head, the ancient woman led her out into the night.

They stood at the edge of a village that the Spanish named *ranchería,* watching the spiraling cooking fires being snuffed out as young families collected their belongings and started off in the direction of the Mission. Soon only the very old and the sick remained. Grandmother waited with the last of the holdouts, and her face held the set of one who welcomed death. A young girl appeared and Maria Inés recognized her mother, tired and hungry, but carrying a cooking basket filled with pozole from the Mission—which she shared with the old ones. Soon the escolte arrived on their tall horses, searching for her mother and for the others who had run away without permission.

Clearly, Grandmother feared for her daughter's safety. The group must be protected; the action of one old person was not important, only the family. With the *soldados* as witnesses, Grandmother made a promise to become one with the white man's god. The soldiers left, but she remained behind. In her own time, her eyes said.

Soon Grandmother walked away from the ranchería, pausing often at the places where the plants had been good to her. She told them goodbye, the plants and bushes that shared themselves so that her family might eat.

From her mat, Maria Inés saw the manzanita, the sage, the wild onions. She watched Grandmother pinch back a leaf and dead-head a dried berry as though tending a child. Under her touch the plants sang their song as if to thank her, a squeak here, a brittle snap there.

"Take with permission. Take with a *please*. Give back with a *thank you*. Sing, pray, talk as you take." These were the things Grandmother taught her. Maria Inés choked back tears as she heard the words. "The plants are the masters. We are the tools." But no more. Her vision continued and she saw that cattle had eaten the leaves and the berries, trampling what they did not devour, and there was little left. She saw the old ones who remained behind with shrunken bellies and hard, hungry eyes.

The dream continued.

The next day, when the sun set behind the western hills, Grandmother stood at the edge of the oak trees that shaded the trail with her few belongings in a burden basket on her back. She gazed at the wooden cross, now darkening in the dusk, the symbol of the new God, and on the other end of the yard, the cannon pointing to the darkening horizon. She felt her limbs trembling and she clung to her charm stone, on a thong around her neck, protecting her from illness.

In her dream, Maria Inés understood that Grandmother did not want to enter the Mission, but neither did she want to die. She wanted to see her son and one day hold the baby his seed would bring forth. Her grandchildren would be the gift the white God would give her in return for her belief. This is what the padres taught.

The old one's head drooped and her shoulders bowed in sorrow. Slowly the shadow returned to the spirit world, leaving Maria Inés alone on her mat, but she no longer felt imprisoned.

On another night, in the stillness of her mind, Grandmother's words entered her ears. Maria Inés began to believe in such things and she listened carefully to the story.

Before the white God came, there was the Great Spirit and he had created many gods—in the skies and mountains, birds and animals, rain and thunder, sickness and health. But the people hungered for more than the Great Spirit and his tribe; they clung to a vision given to the shamans generations ago. One day holy men in gray robes, it was foretold by the elders, would come and teach about the greatest God, the God of all peoples, the Creator of the thunder and the blanket of stars over their chosen valley. The People heard and believed. The vision of the gray robes encouraged them through seasons of drought and hunger. Someday the Great Truth would come, and with it the answer to their fears and longings.

Sleep eluded Maria Inés for many hours that night while her young mind tried to find the path between her world and Grandmother's. For the old ones, the new God was not all powerful because hunger still walked among the People. New sicknesses invaded their huts, and babies died. Many people died who would have lived if they had remained in the oak forest. Some of the people blamed the gray robes, others, the God of the gray robes.

In the waking hours Maria Inés watched the older girls as they threaded the loom with hemp for strength and wool for softness, and wove blankets for sale. Her task was to card the wool into loose strands, then spin the strands together to form a thin rope for the older girls to feed into the loom. As her fingers carded, separated, and cleaned the wool, she studied each motion, committing it to memory for the day when she would be entrusted to weave.

But the sameness of each day's routine, the stiffness of the hemp skirt she was forced to wear, the tediousness of working the spinning wheel with her foot, caused her thoughts to return to Grandmother. In her mind she heard the old one speaking.

"My lips do not pray to the white God when the prayer bells peal."

"My heart trembles with pain when I open my eyes each morning."

"My eyes do not see this place. They stare out into the hills. They see the coyote run free. My ears hear thunder roar. My body sleeps under a blanket of stars. It swims in the river. Now that this old body is baptized, the gray robes will not let it return to the river. My new heart is supposed to be with the white God, but my spirit lives no more."

As Maria Inés spun gray wool into thin strands, she saw her mother sitting beside her, keening like a solitary branch in the wind. Mother was not happy. And perhaps was not unhappy. She just was and wasn't—for her body had joined her dead spirit in the long sleep—but the vision was more real than the world inside the monjério.

Señora Morales was concerned this morning. The annual shipment had arrived and the silk fabric they expected was not among the few chests designated for Mission San Miguel.

"It is the war Spain has lost to Mexico. We have become a burden to our new government who cares only what we can supply to them. They hate us because we belonged to Spain. And Spain no longer feels responsible for us."

She spoke to no one, only the air, for the girls were too afraid to look up from their looms. Suddenly she rose and smoothed her skirts.

"It is no matter. I will sacrifice for the sake of the good. May God see the glory of my actions and take pity on my soul."

She quickly left the room, the echo of her words following her to her quarters. In a few minutes she was back with a silk gown of pale, dusty rose that rustled each time she moved, like the leaves from the cottonwood when they were ready to fall.

The afternoon sun wore a path toward the hills while she sat plucking stitches from the bodice. When the skirts were unencumbered she laid the swaths that showed less wear over the table where the girls took their meals. Afterwards she set Padre's threadbare vestments over the top to measure.

For the next week, every hour that she could spare, she cut and pieced the layers of her skirts into an acceptable altar vestment that would please God. Maria Inés felt honored to be part of such an undertaking. She watched Señora's hand, steady and straight as it made the first cut, and she wondered if she could have sacrificed something so fine, even for God. But the thought quickly disappeared, replaced with the realization that she would never own anything so fine.

On the fourth day of October, Padre Cabot celebrated Mass on the feast day of San Miguel. She was kneeling on the cobblestones before the sun rose, along with the other girls. This was the day they waited for all year. Even Grandmother was there, in the back of the church, watching.

At the moment of sunrise the tender new rays reached through the small window on the east side of the church. They touched a spot on the wall behind the altar, for a few minutes framing the statue of San Miguel in a halo of glowing light exactly as the neophytes and the early padres planned when they laid out the church. The padres knew about architecture, but the neophytes understood the direction of the sun at every dawn, and for one day a year, on this feast day of San Miguel, the miracle appeared to all the faithful kneeling in the church.

When the sun moved on and the light slid farther down the wall, Padre continued the service in his new vestment. The dusty rose pattern picked up the hue of the pomegranates painted on the wall. Maria Inés knelt in prayer, and after she made her sign of the cross, she turned to see if Grandmother was still there, but Grandmother had gone.

Chapter Eight

The routine of daily chores was broken on this fiesta day by a visit to the Wishing Chair. On each visit, Señora Morales told the neophyte maidens about a time, many years past, when Padre Magín paid a visit to Mission San Miguel. A busy and important man, he stopped for a visit from his duties at Mission Santa Clara and, by happenstance, bestowed a blessing on the head of a neophyte girl while happening to promise that she would have her heart's desire. The young woman sat upon the chair and made a wish for a good man as her husband, and it came true. Esperanza had already had her turn. Now it was Maria Inés's turn. She had reached fourteen summers and it was time for her to find a husband.

On her way back from the chamber where the Chair was located, God offered a miracle. She happened to be gossiping with the other girls, the setting sun glinting off the red tiles, at the moment a young Indian man from Mission San Antonio rode by—a proud and handsome vaquero named Lacero. She learned later that he belonged to the Bear Clan. He had arrived to help with the slaughtering and Padre Cabot instructed that he stay to guard the herds from the Yanqui intruders and bandidos who were stealing them in great numbers.

He carried himself with pride because he had ridden from the time he was a boy, and his skill had grown until he now competed with the caballeros at the rodeos. Earlier, she had watched him win the horse race. Today he had helped rope a grizzly and a longhorn bull together for the baiting contest.

Maria Inés shared the bear's indignation. The gruesome event frightened her and she hid behind the other girls, but the event was a favorite among her people. The bout had been bloody and loud. Roars of the animals covered the hoots and calls of the Indians who wagered on the outcome. But a day when neophytes and high-born caballeros alike rejoiced at seeing their brutal enemy defeated. The people were talking about how Lacero had grabbed a lance from the hands of a brave but foolish caballero who moved in close to taunt the bear. The high-born young man had taken a vicious swipe to his brain when the bear caught him in a huge claw, ending in death. Before it could steal the life from another man, Lacero plunged his lance into the heart of the grizzly.

Now that it was over, Lacero seemed shy in her presence. He glanced at her with a particular smile that she returned until the heat in her cheeks forced her to look down at the parched sand. But her heart was not parched. It seemed suddenly lush and teeming with the possibility of life. When she looked up again, Lacero was riding off. She hoped he would turn and glance back, but he shifted in his seat as if he knew she were watching and he didn't care, before his stallion pranced away from her sight.

When Padre Cabot made the suggestion that the two of them marry, Maria Inés had already made up her mind. That night Lacero rode past the monjério. He didn't sing or play his flute for her, but she didn't care because for one moment he looked up at her window.

The wedding took place in the church, with Señora Marcia as a witness. Afterwards, the two of them followed the river on a spirited horse loaned to them by the padre. On their journey to visit Lacero's clan at San Antonio de Padua, they stopped at the old ranchería site where Grandmother had been born. Padre

Cabot had given them permission to be gone until late summer when the crops would be harvested. He had carved a statement onto a piece of rawhide, giving permission to possess the horse, signed by his own hand.

"Why do you have such joy?" she asked one night while a rabbit sizzled above the flames of their small cooking fire, fat crackling in the stillness. Nearby, the stallion munched dry grass. Often it would pause and raise its head to sniff the air until, satisfied, it continued grazing.

"Because life is good."

"All of it? Do you not miss the things the Old Ones talk of?"

Lacero hesitated. "It is said that some of our people live in secret valleys where the soldados do not find them."

Pagans? Could this be? "How do you know this?"

"Brother Owl told me." He smiled.

"Do not laugh at me. Life is better for you. You ride with the sun and the wind. You sleep out under the stars. You soak in the healing waters at the sulphur springs and hope that the grizzly does not share the mud." She pursed her lips together in a way that would make her seem fearsome. "You have more than I do, but do you not wish for another life?"

"I would own my own horse. A herd of horses." He stretched out on the sand and she could feel the heat of his body.

She was weaving a hat for him out of *tule,* but the design was going slowly because he often caused her to lay her work aside and laugh with him in the grass.

"You married me so you would not have to sleep in the mon-jério," he teased.

"Who wouldn't? I wished for you, and one day you wished for me." She traced her finger along the scar on his face left by a grizzly cub he had carelessly surprised while hunting deer. She shuddered at what would have happened if the mother had returned.

"I watched you grow into a plump chicken." He pinched her playfully on her thigh. "One day we will ride to the other side of the mountains and find the Playaños. You can ask them why they hide from the white men that they hate."

"I would like that."

In the distance Grandmother nodded her approval before she faded into the darkness.

When they arrived in the valley of Mission San Antonio de Padua, Maria Inés slowed her steps to absorb the beauty of the simple buildings spread against the valley with their back to the low hills like a baby secure in a mother's arms. Lacero pointed out the long channel that brought water down from the hills to orchards and vineyards, painting the hills with verdant color from rows of figs and olives, apples and pears.

At their approach, swallows swarmed into the air. Distant pings and shouts of hundreds of neophytes made her feel as though she were back at San Miguel, but this Mission was even more beautiful. She remembered the sullenness that some of the northern neophytes showed when they arrived at San Miguel to provide labor in the hard years when there were not enough workers. It was no wonder that they complained of the heat when they arrived at San Miguel. Always she had felt these new arrivals were prideful and angry at being sent away from their relatives, but now that she saw the bustling scene before her, she could agree that this place was grander.

The *Antoniaños* welcomed her and asked many questions about their relatives at San Miguel. She was happy to greet her friend Perfecta, who had married Eucebio, a man with young sons and no wife. Afterwards they made their home at San Antonio. Maria Inés shared only the stories of happiness. There was enough hardship without added worry. She recognized Padre Cabot's brother from his visits, and she answered his gentle inquiries about his brother's health without embarrassment. The air seemed softer in the north, with a gentle evening breeze that came from the west, where deer watched from the river that wound among the oaks.

She woke one morning with a desire to visit the mountains. Lacero agreed. She packed a lunch and followed her husband ten miles into the hills, following an aqueduct that carried water to the orchards.

"How easy it is to water the fields. How do the padres know this?" she asked.

"Padre has drawings in the talking leaves he calls a book. Many such books," her husband answered. "He makes drawings and works beside us."

"Do all Spanish men know the words on the talking leaves?"

"Why? Do you wish you had married one of them, instead?"

She took his hand and shoved him down into the dried grass and they laughed and played together until the sun was far into the sky. Lacero might not know what was written in the books, but he knew other things that interested her more.

One morning she asked to help feed the corn into the heavy gristmill built into the side of a bank and powered by water from an aqueduct that ran a waterwheel. Two neophytes could grind, in the hours before the noon bells rang, corn that would take her many weeks on her metate. The men allowed her to throw a few handfuls onto the grinding wheel. On another day, two men ground wheat into flour. The work was quickly finished, in part because much of the grain had been carried off in carretas to feed the *gente de razón* in Monterey. The neophytes and the padres at San Antonio would have to eat roots and acorns for the winter.

Lacero spent most of his days on horseback, rounding up the cattle for the drive to the place where the slaughtering would occur, where the hides would be skinned and the bodies left for the grizzlies to devour, far from humans. His days were spent in the saddle and he returned each night filthy with sweat, but exhilarated with the freedom of the hills. Each night after they walked to the San Antonio River to cool their bodies in the shady water, she saw his nakedness and felt again her pride that he had chosen her as his wife, especially when she saw the covetous glances that some of the girls cast her.

At night the bonfires burned and the sounds of laughter from men gambling with shells filled the courtyard with energy. No matter how tired she was, Maria Inés loved to watch Lacero throw down the shells and win the admiring hoots of the others. Her husband was taller than most of the other men, his skin lighter. Some of the others teased him and said that he looked like a Spanish youth. He frowned because his mother had also known the relentless harassing of the filthy soldados; her husband was also of mixed blood.

One day, several weeks after they had arrived at San Antonio, when Maria Inés finished digging roots for storage, she walked around the cemetery and saw many mounds of the people who were buried there. Clearly these people had fared no better with the white man's diseases. She traced the outline of one mound and thought about her mother and father, buried in a similar grave at San Miguel. She did not like to think about them because the elders said it was bad to speak or even to recall the people who had gone to the long sleep. Lacero laughed at her when she told him so, but he did not bring up the names of his dead ancestors, either.

When the days of harvest were over and it was time to celebrate with a fiesta, Maria Inés joined the other women in the preparations. Food was scarce this year, the excess already marked for payment of the governor's debts. The air was scented with the smell of roasting beef—always that—but the fruits of the field had been carried off to Monterey to pay the taxes. The kitchen did not exude the smells of honey and cream boiling in a cast-iron pot, sweet *dulces* intended for the children of the nobility. It did not matter that she had never tasted the sweets, Maria Inés remembered the celebrations of her childhood when she and the other neophyte children hung around the cookhouse to smell the scents of the kitchen.

On the day of the celebration she joined the other women in the cool, dark church and listened to the neophytes playing their instruments. An old man, Jose Carabajal, played a violin that he had made himself from hardwoods he found in the forest, after Padre Sancho refused him the right to use the violin belonging to the Mission. Maria Inés felt her eyes fill with tears at the beauty of the old man's music. Better than the smell of sugar dulces, the sound was that of the angels.

The day following the fiesta, Lacero announced that one of the visitors had brought a message from Padre Cabot. It was time to return to San Miguel de Arcángel.

Chapter Nine

Maria Inés's heart raced with excitement as she carried a broom down the corridor and hesitated outside Padre Cabot's quarters. Such a responsibility to tend his room. She knocked, timidly at first, then louder. "Padre?"

No one answered, so she pressed the iron latch and entered.

Inside, a small cot occupied the space along the narrow wall with only a narrow place at the end for a plain wooden desk and a sturdy chair with woven leather straps. The table held a lamp filled with tallow oil from the cattle. She carefully dusted it and returned it to the exact spot. His writing instruments, a candle holder and a sheet of precious paper, lay at a precise angle awaiting his thoughts. A hook held a spare habit that seemed held together by patches. His great, flat-brimmed hat hung on another hook, an indication that he was on the grounds, not in the fields today. She averted her eyes at the sight of his clothing and made a quick sign of the cross. On the table lay his eating implements—a metal plate and utensils with horn handles, and a chipped pottery cup. A long black rosary rested atop his Bible—both worn with use. A battered trunk opposite his bed held his worldly goods, surely nothing of great value. She was curious, but too frightened to open the lid.

Cautiously, she moved her soap-plant broom across the uneven cobblestones, sweeping the dirt that Padre had carried in on his worn sandals. She picked up the last of the dust with her fingers, then wiped the ledge of his small window, trying not to disturb the spider building a web in the corner. Surely Padre did not mind such a small, quiet companion.

Three men approached, taking their time along the corridor while they conversed with heads close together in deep concentration. One was Padre Cabot, the second, a man who had traveled here before, was Señor Alvarado, a good man, and sincere. The third was a stranger who spoke Spanish with the inflection of a high-born man educated in Mexico City. This man demanded answers as though testing the padre's loyalty, his tone rising at the words he wished to emphasize.

"Where has the *wine* gone? Surely thou hast more than the *few* vats I saw in the storage room?"

When they passed her door, Maria Inés fell in behind them, unsure whether she should be witness to such an important conversation, but she was too timid to hurry ahead and too afraid to linger now that her task was finished. Instead she followed at a snail's pace, her head down so that she would not be noticed. The talk continued.

"The drought has claimed the harvest this year." Padre Cabot sounded indignant, but unfazed, his voice strong. "Perhaps next year will be better."

"The Governor cannot pay his debts with *'perhaps'*!"

Señor Alvarado seemed uncomfortable in the other man's presence, but his courtly manners dictated his neutrality. Maria Inés remained silent, listening as the discussion continued.

The tax collector's manner shocked her with its curtness. "Perhaps *thou* wouldst do well to remember that we have been sent for a purpose."

Padre Cabot looked pained. "We have no more wine to send. What remains must be kept for the churches' needs."

The man laughed without mirth. "Thou claim sacramental rights to the *entire* harvest? The new government means to have its taxes."

"Blood from a turnip, Excellency."

"Thou hast the right of it, Padre. But the blood will be *thine*, not ours. Now let us inspect the granaries. Unless thou wishest to claim the contents therein for thine sacramental bread."

"I do not control the rains, Excellency. The wheat heads withered on the stalks this year. Let us pray next year will be better."

"Next year will be too late. Thou art *here* by the government's grace. You *will* provide food and materials for Mexico's needs. If thou does not succeed, the lands will be taken *from* thee and distributed to those who can."

Señor Alvarado smiled uncomfortably. "I understand, Padre, you come from the village of Bunyola on the Mallorca Islands. A land of abundance. Wine enough for the Holy Sacraments and for every meal."

Padre nodded, his head slumped as if remembering.

Maria Inés's heart caught in her throat. The men had halted and were in danger of turning around and seeing her. She turned to peer through a sheepskin window as though searching for something, but the men continued without looking back at her.

"In *my* mind, thou hast traded paradise for hell. From what I have heard, San Miguel *already* claimed the sanity of one monk. Did he not fall into madness within a *month*?"

Padre Cabot pursed his lips and prayed for forgiveness for this idle gossip. "He arrived in August, the hottest month of the year. The first to be assigned here. There was no shelter, no trees nearby. Nothing. The sun addled his brain and he was taken to Mexico City to live out what remained of his life. As you can see, things are better now."

The tax collector sneered. "Interesting. I heard a rumor that he disagreed with the punishment dealt to *certain* unwilling converts and he wrote a letter to his superiors. The rumor was they did not take his *meddling* lightly and shipped him off to Spain with a *feeble* excuse of his insanity." The man inspected his fingers with a satisfied air that Maria Inés detested before he continued in the same self-important tone. "But that is neither here nor there. Surely thou misses Mallorca. Would thou not prefer to return home to die in thy *own* land?"

"This is God's place for me," Padre Cabot replied. "I take no salary from this position. All that I have, I wear on my back. I'm destined to live and die among my people."

The tax collector snorted. "Thou art a better man than *I*, Padre! I fully expect to live out my life on a hacienda of my *own* choosing, somewhere in a more temperate part of Alta California."

"On confiscated lands, perhaps?"

The man smiled. "If God wills it, then it will be so. And undoubtedly with Indian peons who have learned their trades at thy hands." The man touched the brim of his elegant hat with a self-important gesture.

Señor Alvarado made a conciliatory gesture toward the man. "Come, we must talk of other things. Padre Cabot would make a fine neighbor if he would but teach us his method of making brandy from peaches."

"The land is intended for the native people—"

Maria Inés smiled at Padre Cabot's obstinacy.

"—that was the King's promise. In time, each will have a portion to farm."

"In time?" The tax collector's temper flared, causing Maria Inés to cringe in fear of discovery. But the men were too engaged to pay attention to their surroundings. "And when will *that* be, Padre? Spain allowed your people to exceed Padre Serra's estimate by two generations. From your good padre's own lips, ten years and the natives were supposed to be tax-paying farmers. It has been closer to *fifty.*"

Señor Alvarado interjected. "Perhaps the neophytes are not ready to assume such an arduous task. They must learn to practice self-control and moderation if they are to become good citizens of California—"

"Mexican citizens?" The tax collector interrupted. "Surely thou doest not think to make Mexican *citizens* of these people. They best serve the government by serving the haciendas. Nature did not intend the caballero for common labor. A caballero should have no task required of him that he cannot undertake from his horse. Anything more is ludicrous. Let *thine* people hire out to make adobe bricks for the haciendas as they have been doing. Forget about making farmers of them. It is their strength we need, not their voices raised in song."

"Is this your opinion, Excellency, or that of the government you represent?" Padre Cabot asked.

"I fear to agree with you, Padre, for surely our honored guest here shares the opinion of many well-born men in Alta California." Señor Alvarado directed his attention to Padre Cabot and Maria Inés saw the warning in his eyes. "Give a caution to your position here, Padre. It is not as secure as you would have it." Señor Alvarado sighed. "I have been appointed commissioner in charge of secularization of this Mission. Like it or not, the future is coming. I seek your advice on how best to approach the Indians."

"Take it up with them." Padre's voice sounded so weary that Maria Inés was afraid for his health. "If the government is set on its course, the future will affect the people. They should be consulted."

"Thou art an intelligent man, Senor Alvarez. Perhaps thee might inflict some of your wisdom on the good padre here. For his own good. And safety."

The footsteps moved down the walkway and Maria Inés dared to breathe again. She had not understood everything that was said, but she understood the strength in Padre's voice when he defended his people.

She slipped open the door and saw the tax collector's plumed hat turn the corner on his way to the granaries. He would be disappointed there, as well. Padre was saving his grain for the Communion bread. He was no longer even eating his customary slice with his watered-down broth at noontime. Even the pozole was thin and weak, not enough nourishment to feed the many mouths who needed it.

She picked up her broom and hurried to the next room. There was much to be done and fewer hands to do the work. The precious stores of wine and vegetables must be prepared for the endless guests who stopped each night.

It was late and still the governor's representative and his traveling guard sat at the table downing a pitcher of wine from the dwindling vat while their stories grew louder. Maria Inés waited in the shadows, ready to replace a broken pottery cup should one of them break theirs in their drunkenness. The men were of the same sort—puffed with self-importance and without respect for the labors of the Indians. Padre Cabot sat among them, his eyes darting from the meager store of wine to the men who devoured his food, surely wishing he could retire to his quarters. Instead, the men kept him awake with their babble.

"You are lucky your people here do not think to kill you in your sleep, Padre. Other Missions do not have your people's obedient nature. You are to be congratulated."

A shifty-eyed man sneered. "Perhaps Padre puts the fear of God in them and they have lost their spirit."

"The women have not lost theirs. It is a shame the lovely ones are locked up for the night. Is it true you sleep with the key in your possession, Padre?"

"How much would you charge us for the use of that key for

an hour, Padre?"

Only Señor Alvarado seemed to hold regard for the women. "We do well to remember that we are married men with families, my friends. Would you each not kill to defend your daughters' honor?"

Padre Cabot remained silent. When the last man retired, he followed them down the corridor after motioning to Maria Inés to retire.

One of his escolte fell in beside him. "What sacrilege, Padre. God would be pleased if that tax collector slipped on his fancy purple feather and was no more."

"Murder is not in my heart tonight." The words drifted out of the padre's mouth as he stared down the long arcade into the dark. Maria Inés followed the direction of his gaze. Were he a man of violence rather than a man of God, how easy it would be. They would say the man died in a drunken stupor. She noticed that, in spite of his words, he shook with held-back rage. He waited until the last man stumbled away to his quarters before he took his leave, carefully locking his door and hiding the key to the monjério where no one would think to look. In the darkness he picked up his rosary and began to pray.

In the morning he looked rested, but, given his nature, he would need to make confession for the sinfulness of his thoughts. As the cock crowed in the yard, he took a seat at the lower table opposite the tax collector and ate lightly of his porridge. Maria Inés tried to press the last of the kettle into his bowl, but he waved his hand toward the others.

After the meal, Señor Alvarado asked that the neophytes be assembled in the courtyard. With a great deal of confusion, this was done.

Maria Inés was among the women who set aside their cooking pots to follow the others outside. Her husband stood silently beside the others. Señor Alvarado assumed a place on the floor of a stationary carreta and prepared to speak, his voice strong enough that it carried to all the people.

"My name is Señor Juan Bautista Alvarado. I am here today, sent by your government in Mexico City, to proclaim a day of freedom for each of you. If you vote it to be so, from this day forward you and your descendants will be freed from the yoke of servitude. If you adopt the proposed plan that has been offered you, you may go anywhere you wish. Do anything. Each man is promised ten *hectares* of land to farm. Later, we will set up a table and you will each be given title. At no charge. After all, this land belongs to you."

Maria Inés knew what her husband was thinking because his eyes seemed far off: He knew nothing of farming—only horses. She felt her insides churning because she did not want to leave Padre Cabot. She looked around, comforted to see him standing beside the commissioner.

The silence in the courtyard grew ominous.

The man raised his hands as if he were exasperated by what he was witnessing. He began again, gesturing with his hands. "All right then, all neophytes who want to continue living with Padre Cabot—stand to my left. Those who choose freedom and their own land, stand to my right."

To his astonishment, hundreds of Indians moved to his left. She was among them. She heard herself joining the general clamor.

"We want to stay with Padre. He is very good and we love him."

She looked around and saw that a few dozen had moved to the other side to stand next to Señor Alvarado. They stood uncertainly, their eyes on the ground as the others glared at them. Finally they began to move to join the others, leaving the man of the government standing alone. The man seemed to be a decent man. He looked sad, but he didn't understand that this was their home. When he saw their minds made up, he signaled for his horse to be brought forward.

"I believe you are making a mistake. But I will take my report back to my *commadantes* and they will make a decision." He took his reins in his hand and started off toward the north.

Padre Cabot waved off the government men and their guard. The people waited for him to explain what all of this meant, but his face was sad as though he needed to be alone to think. When the entourage was a faint speck in the distance, he mounted his horse. Maria Inés understood his purpose. Whether he was still here in another year or not, the fields needed preparing in time for the next crop or the people would suffer.

In the next days, during their hours of labor and while they were not in prayer, everyone talked about what had been said. Her husband joined the discussion. Padre promised that it would be months before any decision could be made on the matter of secularization. But he warned them that the cost of Commissioner Alvarado's salary must be paid by the addition of more taxes. The people became angry, and she grew afraid when she saw that her husband was one of the bravest to speak up.

"We will have to work all the hours of the sun to pay taxes for this commissioner."

"Maybe it will rain," someone said.

"If it rains, the taxes will take all that is grown."

"We will pray," another added, and Lacero scowled so fiercely that she was afraid for him.

"Do not listen to what the white men say. Watch what they do. This day the commissioner makes Corporal Rios a sergeant. I hear him order our new sergeant to see to the making of many adobe bricks."

"What need has Padre of more bricks?" someone asked.

"Sergeant Rios is required to build a house for the man who comes to be in charge. We will be hired out as laborers and we will have no benefit." Lacero muttered darkly as he ate his small bowl of pozole. "The padre won't even receive the money from our labor, not even enough to save our corn for tortillas."

"How will we eat?"

"The white people do not soil their fine hands," Lacero said. "They demand that we soil ours."

"And starve while we work."

CHAPTER TEN

The sun slid over the top of the east range, laying a thin shadow across the track beneath the oak trees, the morning silent except for the creak of leather jackets, the jingle of sabers and grinding of the carretas rolling deliberately toward San Miguel. At the padre's quarters the carts stopped. In a single movement a dozen men wearing the uniform of the Mexican army dismounted. One studied the courtyard with a disdainful scowl. Upon dismounting he made a great show of stretching his cramped legs as he glanced around. Satisfied that his sacrifice to his government was noted, he bent to adjust his elegant calfskin boots, straightened, and continued toward the padres' quarters.

The rap on the solid oak door, a crack in the stillness, woke Padre Cabot from his exhausted sleep. Thinking it was a ploy to steal the heavy key to the monjério, he slipped it from under his pillow and quickly tucked it into his sandal. Rising, he ambled stiffly to the door.

He blinked in surprise at the man who faced him, but his cordiality did not fail him, even as his limbs trembled with foreboding. It seemed important to make a show of control, if only for the sake of his charges. "Señor Alvarado, what brings you here at such a late hour? Surely there is some mistake. The taxes have all been paid this year. Not an easy thing, to be sure. We have lost many thousands of cattle and horses to the immigrants who have helped themselves to our lands and goods."

105

Señor Alvarado looked uncomfortable. "I am not here to collect taxes."

Were it possible for blood to run cold, the padre's would have, for that was how his body felt, suddenly chilled. But the padre extended his customary courtesy. "In that case, I will show you to a room. You should take your rest. We will speak of business in the morning."

"Would that I could sleep, Padre. I have come with distressing news that I would as soon discharge at my arrival. I am afraid that I arrive at the request of the Mexican government to relieve you of your duties here."

Padre Cabot shook his head, for surely something must be wrong with his auditory function. It was as if the man meant to expel him. "I am a priest, Señor. No one can relieve me of my duties save my bishop—or God."

The commissioner unrolled a script from a waterproof pouch and used it as a pointer. "I am regretful, but as a loyal citizen of Mexico, I have my orders. I must insist that you and any other padres who might be in attendance join me in the chapel immediately. My men will accompany you."

Padre found himself walking barefooted down the arcade toward the church, unable to pause even to don his sandals. The uneven cobblestones bit into his arches with every step. Never had he taken this walk without his footwear, but the thought of protesting was less important than the concerns utmost in his mind. A moment later he was joined by Padre Martin and a visiting priest from the north. They walked single file and waited as the narrow door swung open. No one spoke to break the tension permeating the room.

Inside, one of the soldiers lit the sconces near the door with the tip of his cigar, then did likewise with the opposite pair to provide adequate light for reading. The commissioner unrolled the scroll in his hand and began to read.

"By decree of the Mexican Government, the power decreed to this party by the Republic of Mexico . . ."

Padre Cabot tried to concentrate, but the magnitude of the statement struck him with the force of a death sentence. They were no longer to administer the flocks and the fields—only to minister to the neophyte flock? The Mission and all the others were to be secularized—the lands and properties stolen from the Church. It was premature to return the lands to the Indians, but even more so, a great sacrilege that they would have no guidance from their longtime priests in the matter.

He tried to remain calm, but his sputter betrayed him. "They are not ready for this. They will fall prey to the land-crazed emigrants who are already squatting on the best land."

"Perhaps. But the land is no longer your concern, Padre, only their souls." Commissioner Alvarado seemed embarrassed. "At any rate, the decision was made months ago. It is in the best interests of the people."

"If this is so, then why the stealth in the middle of this night, with only the full moon to guide you as though you were a common invader?"

"Stealth is required if we do not wish to inflame the Indians. Let them find out tomorrow, after they wake."

"And the others?" Padre's voice sounded fragile to his ears "Are there to be no Franciscans left in Alta California?"

"The government is clear in its orders. The Mission system has been abolished."

The commissioner rolled up the parchment and his tone changed to apology.

"In time a parish priest will be assigned, but for now you are allowed to remain. Tonight you must return to your quarters. Speak to no one about this. Remember, no one is above the law. Do not put yourself in danger of insurrection. Take care to hold your opinions to yourself or I will be obliged to report you. You are to turn over any gold or silver in your possession. All valuables are now the possessions of the civil authority. I apologize for the indignity, but I serve at the express direction of my country."

When he hesitated, Padre Cabot felt his arm roughly grasped and an impatient fist thrust into his back. The walk back down the arcade was like that of a condemned prisoner, each step dragging him closer to his destiny. At his door he saw the gleam of the massive key protruding from under his bed where it lay half hidden in his sandal. With the pretence of strapping on his footwear, he managed to slip the key into his pocket while a pair of Mexican soldados rummaged through his trunk looking for gold. He tried to pray, but his tongue could not let the insult remain unchallenged. "If I possessed anything of value I would have sold it by now to feed my earthly flock, Corporal."

The man's grunt was acknowledgment that he had found nothing worth confiscating. Padre Cabot picked up his Bible from the table and managed to slip the key inside without being noticed. He carried it in his hands, forcing the soldados to step around him when they departed. A sergeant of the guard approached, holding his vestments.

"My cope? My chasuble? I will need them to say Mass."

The man shook his head, his eyes hard and set. "It is possible that you have hidden your wealth in the folds. They must be searched."

"Sacrilege! Better that it be burned in a sacred fire than to be sliced through in a hunt for treasure."

"This can be arranged," the sergeant growled. "But you are not allowed into the sacristy. Remain in your personal quarters."

Padre Cabot carried his Bible outside to find the other padres scurrying in a single file from their rooms, their faces ashen with shock. The cool night air heightened the sense of cold. Padre Martin's body shook, whether from fear or cold he could not tell. He moved to his friend's side and said, "Here, allow me to raise your cowl. You will be more comfortable."

A sharp jab interrupted him. "No talking." The guard turned to the other padres. "Into the carreta. Immediately."

Padre Cabot watched his friends being thrust into the back. A moment later they were seated on the rough, bare seats devoid of skins or coverings. The dissolute man at the front shrugged his reins at the sleepy oxen and the cart began to move. From the shadows Padre noticed Enincio, the young Indian boy stationed that night at the door to remove the spurs of late arrivals and to unharness the horses. He nodded slightly, and with his eyes summoned the boy closer. When the boy was abreast of the moving cart, the padre raised his hand to offer a blessing and passed him the key in case he, too, were forced to leave.

From the soldados' quarters, four of the guards streamed out into the darkness, pulling on their trousers and slipping their sabers into sheaths. Sergeant Rios strode up, calling for an explanation.

The commissioner spoke quietly. "A small detachment of Mexican soldados has arrived to aid in the transition. You men are dismissed from duty."

"Where will we go?" one of them asked.

"It does not matter. You may return to Spain if you wish. The Mexican government has no responsibility for you."

"Spain? I've never been to Spain!" one grumbled. "And if I had, I have no money for ship fare. We're owed back wages for a year now. Who pays?"

The man glanced toward his guard. "Apply for land as others are doing. Become a gentleman rancher like Sergeant Rios here. Already many cattle bear his brand. He will not starve."

The men stood about, too confused to protest. Retaliation was impossible, even if they had considered it. They had no powder for their muskets, no lead balls, not even a pair of sturdy boots for mounting a charge. The mustering-out pay that had been withheld each month was locked up in some administrator's strongbox, or more probably, spent on a *baile* or fiesta in honor of the new governor. In the moonlight the men looked ragged and broken.

Padre Cabot stood and watched the horses and carts disappearing. In his mind he traveled with them, helping to strengthen the slumping older padres who were likely spent from shock and exhaustion.

As staunchly as it had arrived, the caravan moved out of the courtyard and rumbled south along El Camino Real, past the sounds of the scattered cattle that remained in the fields, past the vineyard, the dusty sheep in their pasture, the fruit orchards now barren until the next year's harvest. Padre followed them in his mind, his senses attuned to the life he and his brother priests had built from an unpromising land. Now it had been taken from them. He prayed the land would serve the people who held claim to it.

The darkness offered a covering to the sights that would surely break the other padres' hearts if they were to see their homeland in morning's light. The decree mentioned that they were to be dispatched to the nearest seaport. A ship waited to carry his brother-priests back to Spain. They, like him, had little family left there, but they would at last be retired.

Sooner or later, the padres at San Antonio would be subjected to the same indignities. Knowing his brother, the man would insist on remaining behind, even with no way of making a livelihood. His brother was strong and capable, but he, himself, was weary and ill. Perhaps it was God's will that he return to his country before he died. Still, in his heart he was glad he had been spared to remain behind, if only for a few more months.

He pulled his cowl over his head and returned to his quarters, wincing when he stepped on a stone. He uttered no word, either of complaint or of regret. If this were not God's doing, perhaps with prayer, some good would come of it for the people's sake.

A knock on the door sounded a few minutes later, the young Indian boy returning with the key. Padre Cabot held it in his hands and felt his body shaking in misery. He watched as the boy resumed his post before he slowly closed the door, his Bible still in his hand.

CHAPTER ELEVEN

The clanging of the church bells overhead woke Maria Inés. She lay beside her husband and waited for the call to Mass over the clatter that marked the start of each new day. When minutes passed and she didn't hear Padre Cabot's voice calling his faithful to hurry, she abandoned her effort to sleep and began to rouse herself. Already sunlight lit the corner of the room. She heard Lacero stirring on the mat beside her. "Husband, I have something to tell you before the day eats our time together."

"What is this, little dove? Is your nest not to your liking?"

She smiled. "My nest is ready for a lining of thistledown. My egg is hatching."

Lacero turned and smiled into her eyes. He gave her belly a light rub and his eyes roved over her supple belly. "A small egg for such a nest."

"Will you mind if it is a female wren?"

He growled playfully. "It will be a male condor."

She nodded. "A male who will ride the air without moving a feather."

Lacero looked up, excited. "A vaquero? A great rider of horses? Are you sure of this?"

"Your mother had a vision. She has told me this."

Lacero lay back with a look of satisfaction in his eyes. "No brick builder, this son of mine. He will ride like the wind."

Maria Inés wanted to hold on to this moment forever, but her body had urgent needs that must be attended to. She scrambled to her feet, and heard the silence of the courtyard where people should be stirring.

"Something is wrong today, husband. Padre must be ill with fever."

She quickly donned her skirt and tunic.

Behind her, Lacero rolled from the mat and pulled on his new horseman's boots, his most prized possession, made from a calf hide he won in a wager.

"I will go see. Remain here."

She glanced over at the small mat where her mother-in-law slept. Fear pressed her and she nodded. "Be careful, husband. These new men are not to be trusted."

She watched him slip from the room and walk past the two new soldados in Mexican uniforms different from the threadbare leatherjackets of the padre's guard. These men wore new boots and carried shiny pistolas. She was glad Lacero had told her to remain, but she shivered in fear for him.

Behind her, *Oxwe't* stirred, reminding her that the room would trap them if the men were to approach. Maria Inés felt the need to be in the fresh morning air. The soldados had moved toward their horses. The path across the courtyard was clear, but even so she hesitated at her own door, considering.

Under the portico, no pozole simmered in the black, cast-iron kettle as it had for every morning of her life. Worse, Padre was nowhere to be seen. Maria Inés heard hysterical weeping and saw Señora Morales herding her charges, clustered in a tight group, from the monjério toward the spinning room. When they saw the new soldados mounted on fine new horses, some of the girls recovered quickly enough to offer shy glances and giggles behind their hands, but the Señora shushed them and shooed them into the room. The slamming of the door muted her shrill voice and then everything was still.

Señor Alvarado rode in the company of his Mexican escolte,

looking aristocratic and confident despite the fact that he was outnumbered by several hundred Indians. "Do not concern yourself with the padres," he commanded. "Go and eat your meal. We will talk afterwards."

Rather than dispersing, Indians stood in a large group, their murmurs spreading from one to another as they looked about for their morning meal.

"We are to go hungry into the fields?"

"How can this be?"

"Who is this man to speak with such authority?"

Maria Inés threaded her way through the crowd and ran toward the corridor. At Padre Cabot's room she knocked, hesitating at the partially opened door. The room was dark and cool, ripe with Padre Cabot's scent of leather and sweat. His trunk was overturned. Gone, his Bible from the table, and his chair upset as though someone had been searching.

The room seemed abandoned. The hooks that held his coat and spare habit were bare, the bed shoved aside. She glanced around and felt her heart pounding with terror. In one corner, on the cool cobblestone tile that she had swept the previous morning, she saw a glint of light—his small rosary, slid from the table in the confusion. She picked it up, kissed the small crucifix, and returned it to the table before she turned and left the room.

In the courtyard, neophytes milled about. No one seemed to be thinking of their bellies, only the confusion of having no leader to tell them what they should do.

"Where is Padre?"

"Why do our soldados look so sullen? They do not even light their fire sticks."

Maria Inés felt her stomach heaving. She had not eaten and her nausea was more violent than usual. For several mornings she had felt unsettled, but never as much as today. After she voided her stomach contents she felt better. She sipped from the fountain and the cool, clear water eased her.

The elegant Señor Alvarado disappeared into the padre's dining room, leaving the others to wonder who was going to step forward to start the fire under the pot, or to add cornmeal to the water when it boiled.

Lacero was hungry, as well. "I will find something before my belly eats through my skin."

"Each woman must cook for her own family today. We must find something."

"I will hunt for meat."

"Will you be punished, Lacero? Does Sergeant Rios expect you to labor for him? It is hard to know without Padre here."

Without answering, Lacero turned to where an ancient mare stood in the courtyard. One of the neophytes returned from a workshop with a sharp knife and plunged the blade into the horse's neck. Before the men finished skinning it with sharp stones and knives, their women were already hacking off pieces for their cook fires. Maria Inés remembered the *masa* she had ground the day before and soon had a meal ready for her husband. Her small room contained a cooking fire, but they were in too much of a hurry to do more than warm the meat. Lacero sliced off a chunk of horsemeat for her and she accepted it. With her stomach roiling in protest, she raised it to her lips. Nearby, *Oxwe't* picked up a piece and began gumming it with the few teeth that remained. Maria Inés forced herself to eat as well, and found the meat to be surprisingly sweet.

Between bites, Lacero agreed. "We will not starve."

Maria Inés considered for a moment. "The hills are thick with herds."

"Ten thousand horses. Many times more cattle. Many thousand sheep."

"Is this possible? The hills seem emptier with each sunrise."

Lacero frowned. "The white men give our land to newcomers and they drive off the breeding stock. Some kill the vaqueros who give chase."

She looked up, sharply. "Padre will protect us."

Lacero shook his head, dreading what he must say. "A runner came into the courtyard this morning who saw a carreta carrying the padres to the coast. They have gone forever. We are alone now."

"Padre Cabot has not left or I would feel it in my heart. He is still here." She stared at him, tears welling in her eyes. Her stomach rebelled at the food before her, but she knew she must eat for the baby's sake.

After Lacero went out to join the other men, Maria Inés walked to the doors of the church and entered, blessing herself with holy water before making her way to the front. A small sound escaped from the steps leading to the altar. She peered through the darkness and saw Padre Cabot on his knees, weeping. He looked up and his eyes seemed trained on something at a distance. The sight of him so helpless frightened her.

"What time is it? Have I missed Mass? God forgive me, I have neglected my holy oath." He rose and began arranging the folds of his woolen habit. "Come, my child. We must call the others to prayer. The first duty of a priest is to pray."

She returned to the courtyard and summoned the neophytes, but many of them could sense that something was different and they refused to enter. Instead they remained in the courtyard, milling in an uneasy cluster while others made their way into the church. Lacero was among this first group, as was his mother, but Maria Inés turned and entered the darkened church.

When her prayers were over she returned to find a table set up near the front gate. Señor Alvarado was laying his flourishing signature onto scraps of hide that the neophytes could not read.

Maria Inés waited with her husband. They shuffled across the courtyard until they reached the front of the line. She stood uncertainly while Señor Alvarado offered her a kindly smile as though by his efforts he was doing a good thing. Lacero stood with an air of confidence she didn't feel. Perhaps he had a newborn sense of worth knowing that his son would no longer work the fields, but whatever the reason, he acted as though he were a gente de razón. People of reason? Where was reason in the decision they were making now?

"I am a vaquero," Lacero said to the commissioner. "My son will be, as well. What use do we have with land? I would sooner be given a horse."

Señor Alvarado sounded weary. "It is against the law for you to own a horse. Just make your 'x' here. You are entitled to the land. What you do with it is your concern. Sell it if you wish. But I suggest you keep it for your children. It will give you prosperity and a means of income."

Maria Inés looked around the grounds, but she could not imagine the Mission yard looking any different from the way it looked today. In the distance horses whinnied. Closer, the scent of hollyhocks and Castilian roses filled the air. She turned to study the thick wagon track that led south to the sheepfold, and to vineyards already ripe with rich purple grapes. Everywhere the land was fertile and productive, like her own belly. For this man to sit with a paper and tell Lacero that what she saw was no longer possible felt like someone ripping her child from her womb. She bent over as a physical pain gripped her. When she stood again she felt dizzy with fear.

Lacero still stood at the table while the man tapped a fat finger impatiently and glanced over her husband's head as though he were a bug to be ignored. Other Indians pressed close, goaded by the gestures of Señor Alvarado and curious about his words. They discussed among themselves the strange words that the man was saying.

"How can one person own the land? Does it not belong to God?"

"*YaHa,* maybe it is like drinking from the river. You carry the river inside your belly until you piss it out. Maybe this is what the Señor tells us," Lacero said.

The others nodded, their eyes clouded with thought. Maria Inés felt pride in her husband's wisdom. Clearly he understood the nature of owning the land.

"But the People do not piss the earth. We will hurt ourselves."

Someone laughed and she saw Lacero's face turn red.

"Better that we remain together, some growing grapes, others tending the sheep and the gardens."

Some of the others nodded.

"I will rope the cattle and drive them in for butchering. The same with the horses."

Señor Alvarado looked up. "It is against the law for any of you to own a horse. You will be killed for theft."

"Then we will eat them." Lacero's words were brave, but his face turned white. "We will carry hides to the ships. Make trade for what is needed." He tried to make the others understand, but the air filled with uncertainty.

"How will we carry them to the ships?"

"On our heads as our fathers did before the hills were thick with horses," Lacero said.

"There is no more market for hides," Señor Alvarado insisted. "You must grow your own food. Here. Make your marks. It is the law and I am late for my dinner."

Lacero stood at the head of the line, still hesitating. Maria Inés prayed that he would make the right decision.

"What do you wait for?" one of the others demanded.

"Where is this land that you say will be mine?" Lacero asked.

"What difference does it make?" The commissioner swept his hand over a general area on the map that was open on the table.

"Is there water on this land?"

The government man's face flooded with indignation. "The larger parcels have been awarded to those who petitioned for it," he explained. "The governor has many loyal friends. You may have what is left."

A dozen Yanquis waited outside the gate, separated from the Indians as Señor Alvarado had decreed to prevent any pressuring until the neophytes made their mark on the parchment. Lacero made his mark and turned to leave, keeping his head down as he led Maria Inés toward the jostling foreigners. In his hand he carried a scrap of leather that was his deed to ten acres of land. As they neared the gate the clamoring began in earnest. When the first stranger thrust a flagon of spirits at her husband she thought it might be by error, until the man spoke.

"Here's something better than a few acres," he sneered. "I'll make you a fine trade for that deed there."

Lacero shook his head almost violently and Maria Inés was afraid he might strike the white man and be killed. Instead he bent his head and moved forward, refusing to acknowledge the offers of whiskey and gold. Many of their friends were already sitting in the shade with their spirits, taking sips and laughing at the recklessness of the Yanqui traders. Others sported bright coins or necklaces of brightly colored beads. Maria Inés felt light-headed with fear and confusion. Lacero clutched his *documento* in his fist and hurried her through the press of men, some calling out to him in Spanish, others in the Yanqui tongue. One man held a shiny coin in her face.

"Buy yerself something pretty, squaw. You'll be needing it soon enough."

She kept her head down and hurried past, praying Lacero didn't falter.

When it was over and they were safe again in their little room, Maria Inés held her husband in her arms and felt him trembling.

When he rose to join his friends she did not try to stop him.

The next morning, Sunday, the bells rang as they had for over sixty years and Maria Inés joined the other women to watch the carretas of the nearby ranchos roll through the courtyard. Even neophytes who had complained in the past began straggling into the church. Others remained outside, those who still suffered from the previous day's celebration; Lacero was in this group, looking haggard and stiff from many hours spent dancing and gambling, and sharing whiskey with those who had sold their land. She waited on the women's side, hoping he would climb the stairs into the choir loft with the other singers and musicians, but he did not.

When the service ended and worshipers straggled out, the huge black kettle that held the pozole was simmering once again. The gente de razón drifted over to converse with Padre Cabot about the events of the previous week and to offer him food from their gardens. Maria Inés joined the line of women, grateful for her bowl. Lacero joined the men who had butchered a horse while the others prayed and, in defiance of Padre Cabot's rules, were roasting the flesh over a fire of oak coals. Judging from the hungry people waiting for the meat, many were in agreement with Lacero when he said, "The foreigners drive off the herds as though they have the right. We will take what is ours."

A number of young caballeros had grown weary of waiting for their parents to finishing gossiping with Padre Cabot and were putting on a show with their rope tricks for the young ladies. When they tired of roping passing carretas filled with onions, and hens scratching for worms, they rode into the crowd of hungry men with lariats circling. Even the señoritas smiled as they lassoed the steaming horsemeat and dragged it across the sand to the river, accompanied by mongrel dogs that leapt upon the meat and began devouring it.

The Indians watched silently until the young Mexicans rode off before they claimed what remained while kicking at the dogs. Lacero stared at the ruined meat with anger in his eyes. He turned away, refusing to carve out his share and striding instead toward the river. But his wife worried. He had eaten nothing all day and his belly was as flat as a worm. When he turned his back she claimed a portion for them. She washed it in the river before she carried it back to their room, but even though she laid it in the coals to roast, when he returned his pride would not allow him to eat it.

The exercise must have taken a toll on Señor Alvarado because a few days later another Mexican, Señor Ynocente Garcia, arrived with his young assistant to take over as commissioner. Lacero watched scowling from the shadows. He and the others knew this person; the man had spent four years as a soldado in the guard and the neophytes had suffered firsthand from his cruelties. Maria Inés watched her husband and fear gripped her once again. She had not forgotten the humiliation of the ruined meat, but the destruction of food was a small price compared to a diablo who would rule without the padres to temper his cruelty.

Padre Cabot registered little expression about the matter. He seemed unfazed by anything except the condition of his roses in the inner garden. Since the departure of his friends the previous week, Maria Inés had seen him sitting, staring out at the rose garden as though deep in thought. He had not spoken to her, or to any of the others, except through his daily sermons.

After quaffing a quantity of Padre's communion wine, Señor Garcia announced that he wanted more fields planted to barley and wheat, more acres of horse beans and corn to pay his salary as well as the new taxes levied to pay for the governor's extravagances. Maria Inés watched her husband's face, but Lacero remained impassive. The new commissioner waved a dismissive hand toward the church and announced that the Indians were no longer to think of themselves as neophytes. There would be no consideration for education or devotion, for those distractions would interfere with their primary duty to provide a labor force for the new colony. The Indians were not required to attend Mass.

When he finished speaking he assigned a number of men to accompany him to his new home to unpack his belongings. It seemed as though he might stay longer than a month, unlike the last one who had left because he needed to be paid. It would be better if this one left, too, because Maria Inés and the others did not like him.

In the months following, some of her people turned to thievery to feed themselves and their families. Others rode over the hills from the Tulare to harass the foreigners and to take what they could, now that no one remained to protect the Mission. On one occasion, four Yokuts stole several horses, three women friends of hers, and four copes from the sacristy to make sweatbands for their horses from the holy vestments. The escolte had been dismissed without wages, so Señor Garcia forced the Indians, including Lacero, to ride after them to recover the stolen goods.

One day she hurried across the courtyard in time to see a vaquero from a neighboring rancho report that renegade Indians had stolen horses for food and to trade. "My employer, Don Esteban, desires to know what the government intends to do about this."

Señor Garcia's face grew florid. He turned to the Indians who were working in the courtyard and shouted, "This is your fault. You hide thieves among you. How am I to trust even one of you when you are all dirty, thieving dogs?"

He lifted his lash and began slashing at anyone in his path. Maria Inés felt the sting of the whip on her shoulder and she bit off a scream, but others were not as silent.

"Señor Garcia . . . what is the meaning of this?" Padre Cabot came running from his rose garden, his big hat bouncing off his cowl as he huffed across the courtyard. "What does this mean?" He repeated when he could catch his breath.

"It is none of your affair, Priest!"

"God's children *are* my affair. Always. Onto death if it should come to that."

"Then perhaps you should read this."

As Padre Cabot stood with sweat dripping off his chin, the commissioner produced a document and began to read. Maria Inés could not understand all the words, but it seemed the gray robes had been removed from control. The padres who remained were guests of the Mexican government, parish priests, nothing more. The padre's face drained of color and she thought he might collapse.

"From now on, I'm instituting daily lashes. Some of these men are guilty of rebellion and since they will not reveal the vermin in their midst then I will take it upon myself to rout out the insurrectionists myself."

"These poor people are starving. They have no thought except to survive."

Señor Garcia acted as though he didn't hear the padre as he scanned the courtyard for someone he could make an example of. His gaze settled on Lacero.

"You—I saw you cutting up a horse. I intend to teach the others what happens to thieves."

Padre Cabot stood wringing his hands as the guards dragged Lacero off to the whipping post. "That horse was nothing but a rack of bones. Another day and it would have died of natural causes. Butchering it was an act of mercy."

Señor Garcia turned his back on the priest, his face folded into a sneer of satisfaction before he gave a slight nod to begin the punishment. When twenty lashes were administered and Lacero released, Señor Garcia turned to those watching. "Let this be a lesson. Every day I will choose one of you. Take care you do nothing to provoke me or tomorrow it will be your flesh I flay."

Maria Inés followed Lacero back to their room, but she didn't try to help him. His torn flesh was strong and he had survived worse than this indignity. It was Padre Cabot she worried about.

The padre said Mass the next morning, but his sermon lacked its usual fire. Maria Inés was among the group that followed him from the church, pressing close so their voices would not carry.

"Padre, what are we to do? This man has no understanding of our needs."

"It is a time of trouble. We must wait and pray, my child." The padre's words rang as hollow as the cast-iron kettle that no longer held the communal meal.

Commissioner Garcia took the padre aside and lectured him about meddling, with a stern warning about what would happen should the padre continue to speak for the Indians. The following morning the padre shushed Maria Inés when she approached with a whispered concern.

Maria Inés understood little of what was happening, but it seemed to be as Padre Cabot had foretold. Lacero and the others worked as day laborers without pay for high-born families who had received grants of land from the Mexican government. The Indians built adobe haciendas from bricks that Señor Garcia sold them, bricks taken from the Mission's ruined exterior walls, which without any care would soon melt back into the earth.

Many of the new landowners were former soldados from Monterey who were rewarded for their bravery or, in many cases, given land as exchange for wages owed to them. Some of them were good employers and treated their workers with kindness.

The fine haciendas were simply furnished, often with only crude tables and chairs. The new landowners slept on hides or mats on the floor, the same as the Indians because there were not enough skilled furniture builders in California. The Mexican and Indian workers knew how to build with adobe and tile, but they did not have the skills for working with lumber.

Often Maria Inés was hired to prepare meals in kitchens, which were not as well appointed as the smoke-stained kitchen at the Mission, and yet, even in the stifling heat, for fiesta days and Sundays, the high-born ladies wore fine satin and silk dresses with so much embroidery that the dresses could stand alone from their weight. Maria Inés walked many miles to the most remote haciendas, and slept there until she was no longer needed. Lacero was not paid for her labors, but she was allowed to eat the remains of any food laid out for the families. Her belly grew swollen with child, but she did not make allowances for her discomfort.

One morning a fine lady, Señora Vallejo, arrived from the north for a visit at one of the haciendas while on her way to Santa Barbara. Maria Inés spoke to an Indian girl who arrived in one of the five carretas in the caravan. The Indian girl whispered that in the old days, the Señora would have arrived with thirty such carts.

"You are Señora's servant?"

"Of course." The girl's skirt was clean and fresh. "Señora Vallejo has two. We remain near her in case she needs anything."

"Do you tend the children, as well?"

The girl smiled. "She has sixteen children and each used to have a servant for errands and to help with the dressing. But no more."

Maria Inés nodded, puzzled. "Who tends the home?"

The girl's chin lifted in a manner matched by the prideful lilt in her tone. "Señora used to have fifty women for that purpose. Five alone to grind corn for tortillas, seven to help in the kitchen. Five always washing the linens. A dozen sewing and spinning. Each would be insulted if asked to do another's work. It was Señora's way."

"Do you also collect tallow?"

The girl looked as though Maria Inés were a worm in her masa. "Señor used to have three hundred Indians for the purpose of farming and harvesting the animals—all men."

Later, as Maria Inés carried in a pitcher of cool lemonade, she heard the Señora speaking to the ladies of the house. "My Indians were like family. They never asked for money," she said, "nor did we give them a fixed wage. If they were ill, we cared for them. If they had children, we stood in as godparents. If they wished to go to visit relatives, we loaned them animals for their journey. We treated our servants as friends." But her smile faltered. In a whisper she confided, "It has gotten too dangerous in the north. I go to see if it is safer at my sister's home in the south." She looked around to see who might be listening. "My husband fears he will lose everything before this is done. Pray for us."

An exhausted Maria Inés slept beneath a carreta in the grass and rose before the sun in order to draw water from the river. Nearly a week passed before the guests left and she was able to return home to her husband and her small room at the Mission. By then, conditions had grown worse.

Commissioner Garcia had taken revenge on many of the uncooperative Indians, venting his frustration with severe punishments. He was a man of intense appetite and he pursued the women with arrogance and persistence. Maria Inés hid from him as much as possible, and when she found herself in his presence she worked to learn the man's ways so as not to create anger in her ignorance.

Señor Garcia took many cattle for his own use and for his friends. So many cattle were slaughtered that drying hides dotted the plains. Before a trading ship arrived—or when the taxes were scheduled for payment—he announced a *matanza,* a killing time. Lacero was one of six *nuqueuadores.* He rode as fast as his horse could run, hitting each cow on the neck to kill it without stopping until he came to the next, and the next after that. The work was hot and dirty, and he came home splattered with blood, his arm so sore he could scarcely lift it.

The *peladores* followed, quickly skinning the hides. While the valley grew thick with wet cattle skins these Indian men had staked to the ground with wooden pegs, the *tasejeras* followed, cutting the meat into strips for jerking and for grinding.

Maria Inés joined a group of women who carried long knives to cut the fat from the beef to make tallow. When many oxcarts were filled they returned to the work station and began rendering the fat in large iron kettles. When the fat was bubbling and clear, they poured it into *bota* hides they had sewed up, each shaped like a bag. Each bota of tallow earned the commissioner forty dollars, but the money did not return to the people. "When the expenses are paid," he promised, but the expenses were always greater than expected.

At the end of a day spent rendering tallow, Maria Inés's body was rank with the stench of lard and sweat. She summoned Lacero and they walked to the healing place on the river where the sulfur waters and the mud smelled of overripe eggs.

"It is good we don't worry about the grizzly," Maria Inés said as she rubbed mud onto the scars that crisscrossed Lacero's back.

"Yes. The *osos* are in the valley, grunting and fighting over the entrails and the cow heads," Lacero answered.

Maria Inés smiled at the image her husband described. After

the bears ate their fill, the huge condors would devour the remains. The valley would be dotted with the bleached bones and skulls of cattle. In the old days, workers filled the carretas with skulls and piled them onto a stack as high as a hill. Afterwards they used them to build fences around the vegetable plots so animals could not penetrate. But no more. Now the bones would lie on the fields and turn white in the sun.

Señor Garcia called for the matanza more often than the padres had, for he needed to kill the cattle in large quantities to sell hides for his administrative needs. On occasion he allocated a few inferior hides and tallow for the Mission's use. Padre Cabot worked without a salary now, his income diminished until he was forced to eat his meager dinner in the light of the setting sun or, in the winter, by the meager flame of the fireplace because the candle tallow was allocated for sale.

When the hides were dry and the tallow rendered, Lacero and the others drove the carretas to the coast. Instead of trading for clothing and items that had made life easier in the past, the commissioner demanded payment in silver. He decided the Indians should no longer plant hemp or jute because there was little money to be made from it, so the women had nothing to spin into thread for their looms. Maria Inés's skirt and tunic became threadbare, like Padre's habit, but there was no way to replace it unless she traveled to San Antonio de Padua where a field of dogbane still grew in the Milpitas behind the Mission. Without hemp or dogbane, Maria Inés had no wicks for Padre's candles, even when tallow was available.

One by one, the items of common usage became impossible to obtain, even for the high-born ladies.

CHAPTER TWELVE

Maria Inés rummaged through the root storage in the Mission quadrangle and managed to find a number of withered potatoes. Sifting damp sand through her fingers, she discovered some carrots and a pumpkin squash from the summer harvest. Concealing them in the folds of her worn skirt, she hurried back to the kitchen.

Lacero returned with a small tree squirrel he had lured with a walnut buried beneath a tree.

"Only a few more months and the orchards will be ripe. It has been a wet winter. The trees are fat with buds."

"As are you, wife," he teased. "It won't be long."

Her face heated and she turned to finish cooking her meager meal. The sound of horses and shouting distracted her from her upcoming birth.

A rough band of men had arrived, travelers on El Camino Real who needed lodgings for the night, and it was the task of the Indians to feed them. Maria Inés glanced at the small portion of lamb meant for the padre's dinner and considered ways to stretch it to feed a half-dozen more. The padre would be gracious with his food, but she was angry for his sake. Señor Garcia made a decision to join them as well, possibly because he was bored with his own company and longed for the conversation of worldly men.

After the boiled lamb and rice was served, the men brought out their flasks. Likewise, Señor Garcia brought out his own wine, which he offered to the visiting priests in scant portions. The rest he kept for himself while Padre looked around apologetically at the guests gathered under his roof.

"I would offer you a libation," he began, "but I dare not squander my meager supplies of wine. With the governor's new regulations I have become accustomed to having a glass only on feast days and holy days."

Señor Garcia glanced up from his meal to offer a slight toast of his chalice. "A worthy forfeit, Padre. Offer it up as a sacrifice. It will temper the sinful spirit. Isn't this right?"

The padre's face darkened, but he kept his peace. The company of the men was tedious to him; Maria Inés noticed the way he drummed his fingers on the table while attempting to listen to one in particular. This traveler acted as the group's leader. He loudly proclaimed to the visiting priests, who had arrived earlier in the day and sat in modest silence, that his name was Isaac Graham.

In the next hour he claimed the attention of the others with tales of his former adventures on the high seas. Sometimes one of the other men added to the conversation, but always Señor Graham's story was more boldly told. Maria Inés found him obnoxious and foul-tongued. Señor Garcia apparently liked his company, for they exchanged crude jokes and stories that made her ears burn.

One of the visiting priests, an old man who kept his napkin in his sleeve, refused all her offers of assistance, brushing her away with a swipe of his hand. "Did you hear of the troubles in the north?" he asked Padre Cabot over the voice of Señor Graham. The old priest cocked an inquiring eye at the commissioner as he spooned his meal into his horned cup—the meat, the dessert, even the dregs of spirits offered by the visiting men—and stirred them together. "Señor Vallejo is unable to provide written title for his land grant from the King. The document was lost—or never written."

"Strangers are taking over the old Spanish land grants. Squatters. Americans, mostly. Disappointed miners from the Sierra Nevada. They think they deserve what they can grab from us Mexican interlopers," one man said.

"Maggots," another groused.

"Ah, but Señor Vallejo is a generous man—even in his trials," Padre Cabot added.

"He has given many people their start on his land," the old priest agreed. He began eating from his cup with a spoon he carried with him.

"Heard he lived like a king in the North Country at one time." The rough man, Graham, sounded as though he admired Señor Vallejo.

"But kings fall. He is simply the next," his traveling companion added. The talk continued around the table as the men grew drunker. Maria Inés made caution to remain silently in the corner until she was needed.

"Has ever goodness prevailed over the jealousy of an enemy?" The old priest looked up from his cup.

The rough man sneered at the spectacle the old man was making of his food. "Are you preaching anarchy, Priest? I heard they shipped your kind off on a ship. A word in the wrong ear and you could find yourself aboard one as well."

The priest sat mutely wiping his spoon with his napkin while Maria Inés trembled from the tension in the room. When the spoon was clean enough to suit his needs he returned it to the pocket hidden in the folds of his robe, and the napkin to his sleeve. The only sound was the clinking of pottery as Maria Inés cleaned away the dinner dishes.

After a few minutes Padre Cabot was unable to restrain his yawn. "I have been up since daybreak. Poverty takes a toll on the aging body. I am fortunate to endure the pace at my age."

He stood and the others clambered to their feet, as well. Some of them glanced around uncertainly as though looking for a suitable place to retire. Señor Garcia took his leave to sleep off his drunkenness at his own home. Padre Cabot indicated by his nod that Maria Inés should leave before the men gathered their wits.

On her way back to her quarters, Maria Inés saw the men securing their bedrolls beneath the portico. One stared at her with a penetrating look that made his intentions clear—even though her belly was swelled with pregnancy. Frightened by his boldness, she put her head down and hurried across the courtyard.

She hoped the padre would not be disturbed. His health had broken with all the changes of the past months. He had tried arguing with Señor Garcia for the Indians' sakes, but each time his offer of advice was refused. *A dead man who woke each morning* was the way her people described him. Each day he paced the arcade, fingering his beads, his head down, his eyes reflective. The only triumph he had achieved was the right to retain the key to the monjério. He felt a personal responsibility to the young women; a system copied from the upper classes in Spain, he claimed, that had served their society for hundreds of years. He could not allow the key to rest haphazardly on a hook in some distracted commissioner's keeping. The key still slept under his pillow each night.

The drunken laughter of the men under the portico concerned her. The air was chilled and they had drunk much. She offered a prayer that they would not harass the Indian women tonight, but the sound of bawdy shouts and hoots followed her as she hurried to her little room.

She gratefully slipped onto her *tule* mat and after many minutes, managed to sleep. Her dream of the forest was broken by the loud rending of split wood, followed by hysterical screams and pleading. Beside her, her husband bolted awake and listened.

"It is the monjério! The Yanqui dogs have broken in. The girls!" He rose to his feet and ran outside, unsure what to do. The soldados had been discharged from their duties, the barracks empty. Outside, Indian men ran toward the maidens' quarters where each had a sister or cousin in residence.

At the corner, the foul-mouthed Señor Graham held a pistola against the breast of a struggling young girl while the others cowered, too frightened to move. Frightened Indian men crouched in the courtyard, uncertain whether to close in. Graham saw them milling in the dark and he shouted, "Come closer, you peons," the violence of his tone adding to the confusion. No one challenged him and, one by one, his own men charged into the room, laughing and unfastening their trousers. Inside, the screams continued.

One of the younger Indians climbed the bell tower and began ringing the bell.

After what seemed like an entire night to Maria Inés, the marauders slipped out the door and returned to their makeshift camp, laughing and joking as though they knew no one remained at the Mission to challenge them. And they were right. Not even Señor Garcia appeared with his old flintlock. His house was within sound of the bells; it was possible he did not hear, but either way, what could he have done?

As soon as the men vacated the shattered quarters, Maria Inés followed her husband and pushed past the broken door. Some girls were crying. Some sat with shocked expressions of horror on their bruised, bleeding faces. She wrapped a young girl in her arms and turned to see Padre Cabot standing at the door, his expression broken and defeated. In his hand he held the key he had guarded these twenty years.

Maria Inés spent the rest of the night wiping away blood and tears. She had no answers for the plaintive questions the girls asked. Some, even the ten-year-olds, would carry a baby after tonight, but a problem for another day.

In the morning the travelers calmly made preparations to leave. Padre Cabot commanded the cooking fires not be lit until the men were gone. For the first time in Maria Inés's memory, the Mission did not provide their guests with a morning meal. She watched silently as they stowed their gear onto their horses and started north—after making sure everyone saw the barrels of their pistols and heard their jeering laughter as they rode away.

"Tell the señoritas not to pine for us. Maybe we will be back one day," one of the men called from his horse.

"Remember us. And be happy no one was harmed. Just a little innocent fun," another added with a laugh.

When they were gone, Padre Cabot remained in his room, refusing food and water for the next days. Lacero rode the padre's fastest horse to San Antonio to share what had happened.

On the following Sunday Padre Cabot's brother arrived from Mission San Antonio. In his sermon he announced that he would be assuming his brother's duties. "Padre Juan will be retiring to San Luis Obispo. He is in frail health and wants to spend his last days in the gardens."

It seemed to Maria Inés the heart of the Mission had broken.

The carreta carried Padre Cabot along the dusty trail while neophytes ran alongside for a league or more. They would have run farther, but Padre turned and dismissed them with a blessing. *"Amad a Dios, hijo!"* Love God, son.

Maria Inés's eyes filled with tears as the padre waved for them to cease following him and return to their homes.

Without the padre to harass, Señor Garcia seemed to take even less interest in his responsibilities. At the end of a year he left because he had not been paid and Señor Pico took his place, but he left as well and another replaced him.

Carretas arrived to carry off many of the furnishings and kitchen wares, spinning wheels, and boot-making forms for men who produced documents that held their claim to the goods. They loaded wine barrels and the padre's brandy stores. Others arrived with hastily scribbled notes signed by the governor, pledging his gambling losses against the most valuable items. The wine press disappeared along with harnesses for the oxen, carts, and animals. Plows and draft animals followed until nothing remained for the neophytes to tend the fields with. In a single day, over a hundred mules were taken.

Strangers wandered through the Mission rooms looking for anything to carry to their barren homes. Maria Inés pretended to dust what remained, sometimes hiding small objects in her skirts to prevent their theft, but despite her efforts, most of the people found something of value. She was glad Padre Pedro Cabot locked the church against those who would steal the sacred objects.

One day, as Lacero watched with an impassive face, a group of men claimed the tame saddle horses. Maria Inés pressed her arm against his and felt the strong beating of his heart. His eyes remained stormy as he led her through the courtyard to their quarters. They had no spoken plan to return to their rooms, but the world seemed unfamiliar and the only place they knew was this small place. Once inside she saw that behind his brave face, her husband looked frightened.

"What troubles you, husband?" She tried to make her voice seem strong for his sake, but her words sounded shaky.

"My horses are not at the river where I hid them."

She understood he spoke of the horses he loved the most, the ones he rode in the fiestas and, most often, won the wagers with his trick riding. Her heart sunk with despair. The three horses were his life.

"I saw saddles carried off before the sun was high," he said. She nodded. She had heard the carretas leaving. "I tried to find Padre, but he was of no use."

"He can do nothing for us. You know this."

"They are payment for the governor's gambling debt, he said."

"Let it go, Lacero. There is nothing we can do, either. It is finished."

"That is what the white man said when he took them." Her husband's eyes were dark with anger. She moved nearer to comfort him—and to feel his strength.

"What will we do, husband?"

"There is nothing." The words halting and defeated. "As soon as they have what they want, the strangers will leave. The people will remain. The land belongs to us. We are the people of the oaks. You will see."

Afterwards, she lay on her mat and turned to face the wall while she tried to drive out the sound of men pulling the huge bell from its mounting. She heard the thud when it hit the ground and she wanted to weep. How would her people know when it was time to eat or work? She thought of everything that had happened in the last week and it was more than she could bear—as if the world had ended for her. Maybe this was the way Grandmother felt when she had to leave her village—strange and alone. Eyes closed, she tried to summon a vision of Grandmother, but the spirit did not come. After a while she slept.

CHAPTER THIRTEEN

Maria Inés woke from a restless nap and tried to identify the sound that had roused her. She was glad it wasn't the sound of gunshots trying to frighten the Indians into leaving. For many months they had tried, but the people had nowhere to go. Only a few days earlier, two Yanquis had killed an Indian boy running through the sagebrush hunting rabbits.

Lacero had taken her to visit the small piece of land they had been given, but it was far from water and the trail to reach it went through another man's land and he stood glaring at them with his long gun across his chest. Without fencing or a plow, the land was worthless to them. Already the man's horses grazed their grass, but it was of small importance because Lacero had no horse, anyway. Most of the Mission horses had been stolen, driven off by fierce-looking mountain men to New Mexico for sale to the American army. He was lucky to find an ancient mare he led, at danger to his own life, to a cool sycamore tree on the bank of the river where he tied her in the shade.

"We will be killed for possessing a horse, husband. The white man has warned us."

Lacero gave a grunt. "They will kill us if they want to."

"Husband, I am afraid for you."

"I am a vaquero. Where is my life without a horse?"

Maria Inés turned her attention from her immovable husband to his growling belly. Her baby stirred inside her, reminding her they would soon need food—and a place of safety.

That night Lacero reconsidered. The ancient mare would not make it a single kilometer. He and the other men killed the horse and spent the night butchering it and the women sliced it into strips for drying while hungry dogs fought each other for the entrails. She helped until the end, when she was happy to return to her room and collapse on her mat. The baby was heavy now and she was tired. The meat would be good for the baby, one less thing to worry about. She was almost asleep when Lacero returned with armloads of salted beef strips. She smiled at the muffled sounds he made as he hung the strips to dry. It was good to hear him so happy, she thought as she drifted off to sleep.

A few days later she woke from a troubled dream with an empty stomach and tried to discern the sound that had awakened her. It came from the plaza, the rasp of men tensely shouting to each other from their horses. Her heart raced with fear. Perhaps it was Señor Graham and his men returning to force their way into the monjério, although the room was empty now, many of the girls hired out as servants on the haciendas to bring in money for the commissioner's salary.

Whoever it was, their hoofbeats did not head in the direction of the priest's apartments, but instead, toward the corrals. Maria Inés pushed open the stiff cowhide hinges of her door and saw a trio of men with lit torches setting fire to the corrals where the poorest of the Indians lived. A group of ragged, hungry children ran out from the smoke, crying and calling for their mothers as the inferno grew. A ragged scream pierced the morning air, followed by silence and the stench of burning flesh.

Maria Inés stood frozen as the men turned their horses toward the orchards, catching first one tree and then another with their torches. Soon the olive trees were ablaze, spreading to the apple and quince trees that would have provided food for many families this winter.

The men rode down one row and back up the next, working in silence to fire the orchards. Then they turned to the vineyards.

"Let's see you hang around when there's nothing left to eat, you damn Diggers!" one of them shouted in the language of the Yanqui devils. He threw his torch inside a neophyte room and rode off laughing. Maria Inés heard the family stomping the fire out as it engulfed their mats and the rags they had collected.

"Please, God, save us." The prayer on her lips was silenced by her husband's curse.

"We leave today." His voice was terse with determination. "We will not die like rabbits."

"But what if Padre Cabot returns?" she whispered.

She had never seen her husband so angry. "He is dead."

"He is not. I would know in my heart if this were true. He is at San Luis Obispo de Tolosa, with his roses. But he will return."

"He is dead to us." He turned away from the children who were crying for their mother. "We return to Mission San Antonio. We will be safe there."

She kept her head down as she gathered her things. Part of her was glad they were leaving this place of sadness. With no promise of food from the fields, many more would die now. The men outside had destroyed their last hope.

"Where is your land documento? You have kept it safe?"

Lacero grunted. "It is safe. Wait here. I will return before the sun begins to eat the mountain."

Now that he had made up his mind, he was in a hurry to leave.

Maria Inés waited in silence. It would do no good to speak of her fear for her child, already stirring in preparation for its birth. There was a padre at Mission San Antonio who could baptize her baby. Praise God she could find safety in the beautiful valley of the Antoniaños.

She was ready when her husband returned on the back of a buckskin mare he had acquired from somewhere. He did not tell her and she did not ask. Instead he pulled her up behind him and waited as she awkwardly adjusted the burden basket she carried on her back. The horse moved a few paces and she swayed with the unfamiliarity of riding astride.

"Hold on to me," her husband said, his voice smiling at her awkwardness as she stretched her arms past her huge belly and held on.

Afternoon blended into evening as they rode out, following the river to avoid the road. The hillside on the other side of the river was bare of cattle, the silent grass glinting in the sun. From an oak nearby Maria Inés heard a woodpecker sawing a hole in the trunk to store its acorn. Nearby, a titmouse rustled in the branch before dipping down to swallow a beetle skittering along the trail. It was as though the land was returning to the people.

Lacero nodded toward the bug. "Vermin. This is what they call us. As if we are worms eating their grain. Diggers—because we dig roots for our meal. It will get worse when more Yanquis come."

The day had held enough sadness for her. Overhead, the titmouse scolded Lacero as well. She sucked on a stone to make herself forget her hunger until they halted alongside the river, at a spot where strangers would be unlikely to find them—or worse, the horse.

She slid off the horse and rubbed the soreness from her thighs while she found a place to relieve herself. Afterwards she pulled out a ration of jerked horsemeat and mint leaves she picked from a bush. When they finished their stomachs were not full, but it was enough. She realized it had been days since she had eaten a bowl of pozole.

A magpie zigzagged overhead with a bug in its bright yellow

bill. She looked around for an oak and found one with a crop of acorns. Acorns. She remembered the old women leaching the bitterness out and grinding them into meal. The padre had not encouraged the women to waste their time in pursuits of the old ways, but many had prevailed. A good thing because now the gardens were dead and the forest lay thick with nuts.

Suddenly she heard the ragged shouts of two men calling to each other across the sagebrush. She looked up and saw one of them on his horse, pointing his rifle toward her and her husband. Lacero saw it, too. There was no time to mount, but maybe the men would be satisfied with the horse. A shot rang out and he shouted for her to run.

"Take off your shirt so they do not see you. Disappear into the brush. Run."

She skimmed out of her clothing and crouched among the sagebrush while another shot rang out, followed by the sound of swearing. A third shot and the sound of Yanqui laughter. Lacero scowled at her, his face black with fear, and pointed for her to run in the opposite direction. She kept low, protecting her belly as she zigzagged through the brush, away from the guns. Lacero was somewhere to her right, running like a jackrabbit, she knew, even though she could not see him. When she could run no farther she crouched into a tight ball, under the largest of the sagebrush so she was well hidden. Naked, she listened for the sound of Lacero's running, but all she heard was the sound of another shot, then another.

In her confusion, it seemed as though footsteps trod all around her. She heard the shout of a man when he found her burden basket and his pleased surprise when he found the jerky she had spent days preparing. After a few minutes the footsteps were replaced by the sound of horse hooves leading away.

Lacero!

Her breath caught in her throat. She waited until the magpie began singing again before she emerged from her burrow. Standing, she uncoiled herself, limb by limb, amazed the baby still moved inside her.

"Lacero?"

She whispered the name, afraid the men would hear as she moved in the direction she had seen him run—crouching down so the sagebrush would hide her. Ahead, she saw her husband's body sprawled in the dirt, one arm extended toward the knife he had pulled from his ragged scabbard. From a gaping hole in his chest, frothy red blood gurgled out in slow, even spurts until, slowly, it ceased and his body was still.

She froze and felt her heart pounding with such fear she had no room even for sadness. Instead of crying she clapped her hand across her mouth to keep silent. Lacero had promised to bring her to safety and he had left her. Gone, too, the horse. She felt the emptiness of the vast valley in which she stood, alone for the first time in her life. Without warning her legs crumpled and she fell to the ground beside him.

When she opened her eyes again, she knew his spirit had left his body. She tried to rise and felt the pain of her cricked neck. Her stomach felt dead, but she was too weary to fear for her baby. With dull, stiff movements she managed to stand and, with effort, moved away from her husband.

The river was near. She cupped her hands and filled them again and again with sweet water until she felt her strength returning.

Flies clustered around the bullet hole in Lacero's chest. She brushed her hand across him and sent them scattering, but each time they returned. He needed to be buried. She knelt in the sand and began digging a depression with a stick. Through the long night she continued, and when it was deep enough, she dragged him inside and filled the depression around his body with pieces of driftwood and sticks. Sand followed. She searched for rocks from the riverbank, but found few and so filled his burial hole with sand.

The sun was climbing across the valley by the time she finished. The grave was shallow, but it was the best she could do. Brother bear or brother coyote might find him, but she had done her duty—if the animals needed food for their own journey, then so be it—her husband's soul was already with God, all that mattered. Still, she needed to pray for his soul. Her fingers clasped at her neck and at first her frantic fingers did not find what she searched for. But God was with her—her rosary hung around her neck, tangled in the locks of her hair. She pulled it over her head and knelt. As she began to pray she felt her body relax from the terror of the past hours. Her tears flowed and her throat was thick with emotion, but her words were strong.

"Lacero—husband. You are with God."

She wanted to say more, but suddenly her grief dissolved into numbness. Silently, she finished the beads and hung the rosary carefully back around her neck. The sun was high in the sky. She stood and began to search for her clothing, retracing the trail of terror that had taken her from her husband's side. When she found the skirt and tunic lying limp in the sand, she stood staring, unwilling to touch them. It seemed another lifetime when she had dropped them. Slowly, reluctantly, she pulled them on and the rough, ragged fabric against her skin was a reminder that at least part of her still lived. With nothing else to occupy her, she began following the river.

By nightfall she was weak from lack of food. Her skin was raw from mosquito bites, her feet torn and sore from the hot sand. Too weary to continue, she burrowed a bed in the sand. She longed to lie down and sleep, but for the baby's sake she had to eat. She searched along the riverbank for an overhang where a fish might be hiding. When she found one she crouched motionless, not moving until the sun had set and the night birds had commenced their songs, but still, nothing. Finally, when she could not keep her eyes open any longer, she filled her growling belly with cool water and returned to her bed in the sand.

In the night she woke and struggled to her feet to empty her bladder. Above, the North Star pointed the way to Mission San Antonio. For long minutes she stood, trying to decide her course. Without Lacero she had no reason to go forward, but she had nothing behind her, either.

Her sleep was filled with fearful images as she wrestled with decisions of what she should do. The moon was low in the west when Grandmother appeared. The spirit woman remained still while the air around her swirled like blowing sands, but her hand pointed to a place just beyond a patch of brush where the burden basket was lying on the bank. Found. Maria Inés cradled it in her arms and felt herself drifting into peaceful sleep.

Upon waking she smelled the pungent odor of wild onions. Her mouth salivated as she tore loose a handful of onion bulbs and raked off the outer leaves, working with both hands. She stuffed one into her mouth and chewed it into small bites, then grabbed another, not waiting to taste until the ache in her belly abated. Farther up the creek she found chia seeds, and seeds from the bunchgrass growing in clumps near the water. And, beyond that, willow to ease her pains.

When her belly was sated, she struggled to pull her burden basket on. She started onto the trail, but she took only a dozen steps before she halted. From a hazy image in a cottonwood tree Grandmother was indicating an ancient trail through the undergrowth. On the bark of the tree was emblazoned a cross, burned in the wood by Padre Serra to mark the trail. From out of nowhere a breeze picked up, rattling the dry grasses until they seemed to be whispering directions. Grandmother led the way and she followed, and with every step some of the heaviness left her body. Grandmother was with her. She was not alone after all.

The trail wound through the sagebrush near the river where small rabbits and mice had never seen a human and the sight of her with a rock in her hand caused them to merely hesitate in curiosity, not to flee. Her aim was true, and before she touched Lacero's knife to skin the rabbit, she thanked God for the successful hunt. The remembered taste of roasted meat made her mouth water, but she dared not risk a fire. Instead, she ate it raw.

In the morning she finished the rabbit and found a handful of seeds, as well as another onion. She scraped the rabbit skin clean and hung it over a rock to dry, a gift for the baby. When her strength returned she followed the river south. The golden hills trapped the late autumn heat and her feet caught on pebbles. She had watched Lacero make his boots, but she had not thought she would need the skill—the padre assigned men to make the sandals and boots. Now she would need to learn.

The sound of horses drove her into the bushes just before a trio of hard-looking bandidos raced past, crouching low on their horses to ease the burden of the bulging sacks in their saddlebags. The one in front she had seen hiding in the trees outside the Mission many times, waiting to evade the Yanquis riding in pursuit of him. She recognized him from the times that he stayed at the Mission and took advantage of Padre's kindly manner. His name was Santos, but the people called him El Lobo for his wolfish ways. It was said he would not hesitate to use his gleaming knife blade on a man, as much for the exhilaration of killing as for the handful of gold coins the man might possess. She crouched, trembling until the sound of their horses disappeared on the old Indian trail. She would need to keep a sharp eye in case anyone was following, one group of men as dangerous as the other to an Indian girl alone.

The world had become infested with vermin of the earth. Padre Juan Cabot must be weeping for the sins against his people. Surely he was praying because God had pity on her today and she met no other riders.

Sundown brought out bats hunting for mosquitoes, and later, owls on hunt for mice. She listened for the rattle of a snake on the sand, but she heard nothing. For long minutes she sat motionless, hoping to catch a fish, but she had nothing to catch it with, only her hands, and each time she tried her belly made her clumsy and slow. The morning meal had been satisfying, but many hours ago.

A fox entered the clearing to drink from the river where she crouched, but before she could react, it bounded off. She lowered her rock and her ears caught the sound of Lacero laughing at her clumsiness. Stiff and discouraged, she drank from her cupped hands and waited.

When she finally gave up the idea of finding food she began walking again. The Mission was only a few hours ahead—already the valley walls narrowed and the hills grew steeper. She found a field of mustard planted by the first missionaries to mark El Camino Real. She pulled off a handful of yellow flowers and stuffed them into her mouth, chewing the tangy, peppery heads. They would satisfy her hunger tonight.

It was midnight when she saw the low buildings of the neophyte housing against the rising hunter's moon.

With burning feet and a nagging backache she slipped into the darkened room she had shared with Lacero. Something near the door grunted and shifted so quickly she was thrown off-balance. A man rose with his hand curled into a fist. "Who goes there?" he growled, the words the soldados used.

"It is Maria Inés. Please. Have pity on me."

"Maria?" In the darkness her friend Esperanza's voice interrupted. "We thought you were gone. You and Lacero. He is here as well?" It was not a question, only good manners.

"I will tell you tomorrow. Now I must sleep."

"We also have news to share. Tomorrow, then."

CHAPTER FOURTEEN

Maria Inés woke with a nagging backache that didn't ease as the morning passed. She spent the hours telling her friends about Lacero's death and, mercifully, found that reliving the terror took her mind from the contractions wracking her body, even if her mind remained sore and bruised. By noon the baby began its birth.

"Lacero," she whispered each time a contraction occurred. She was glad the old ways had passed and she did not have to fear the ancient gods if she used her husband's name. His name was written on her heart.

When she knew it was time, she whispered, "Get a knife."

The baby was born when the sun began its path across the sky. It seemed strange, not having the bells to signal the hour of prayer. She felt alone as she labored in the room that had been hers, but was now shared with another family. Solia, the woman who had become both midwife and confidante to the remaining women, arrived in time to deliver the child—a healthy boy.

"What is to be his name, little mother?" Solia asked as she handed the small bundle to its mother.

"Miguel Lacero," Maria Inés answered, her eyes clouded with tears. "We call him Miguelito."

The midwife nodded approvingly. "May God shed tender mercy on the child. Let him never forget the man whose name he carries." She smiled and began swabbing the baby with steamed salvia leaves cooled to lukewarm. "I knew your husband. I am sorry he leaves you without seeing his child. He was a good man."

Maria Inés's sadness eased when the baby began squirming. "This one will be a vaquero like his father," she murmured, "already anxious to leave his mother's arms."

"California will be a good place for him. A better place, God willing. Let us pray that they return our priest to us. The child can't be baptized without one." Solia turned to collect her things.

After she left, Esperanza stepped forward with an abalone shell filled with water. "You are safe here. My husband goes to find food. Do not worry. He will return with enough for many days."

Maria Inés's spirit did not respond. Could it be only a few days since she had lived here with her husband? The room still smelled faintly of Lacero's leather boots, but how could that be? She had buried them with him so he would be warm in his long sleep. Now only his scent remained, and only that in her memory.

She drifted to sleep and saw Grandmother watching from the corner.

She woke to a single rooster crowing and to familiar pangs of hunger. Desperate Indians and travelers had taken most of the hens, and those remaining spent the night roosting in the trees, but they came down to scratch for grain and to lay their eggs in the dry grass. Perhaps one of the children would find her a fresh egg.

Esperanza returned with a bundle of grass for pounding. She had picked a clump of salvia, which she used to bathe the baby, and made the rest into tea with a steaming rock in her basket. Maria Inés was grateful. The tea soothed her birthing pains even if it did not quench her raging hunger.

Esperanza's husband Jose Toma returned with a possum. He

also carried a chunk of fat. "For candles."

The thought of candles reminded Esperanza that she had seen a chunk of lye soap behind a table in a workshop. "While the meat roasts, I will go search."

"We have nothing to scrub," Maria Inés said. "Everything is on our backs."

Esperanza looked up and her face grew sullen. "I will find a pile of wool and weave a cape for the cold."

"How? The looms have been sold." Maria Inés saw her friend's frustration and wished she had not spoken. "We will eat well tonight. Your husband is a good hunter."

Esperanza nodded. "I will return with the soap. We will make a trade for something we need."

When she took her baby for its first walk Maria Inés found a discarded whiskey flagon in the grass where one of the neophytes had dropped it when he finished drinking up his land price. She hid it in her skirt and continued walking; perhaps she could trade it for something more useful. Inside one of the workrooms, hanging from a rafter, she found a length of cowhide strip holding a cluster of dried chilies. The strap would be useful in securing the burden basket cradle to her back.

In the garden women dug for onions and carrots. "We must leave some for seed."

"You leave your portion. My family is hungry." The woman who spoke was not a bad person, only doing her best for her children.

For those who chose to stay, the commissioner had assigned longer hours of labor. Several girls were making adobe bricks to sell. The sun was intense, but the girls found no relief from the heavy lifting. All day the work went on. The people had to find their own food when they were finished with their new quotas. No one was excused, even for childbirth. Maria Inés lashed her baby into the burden basket she now used as a cradle and slipped the headband across her head before she joined the others. She didn't feel weariness or heat; her mind was dead to feelings of misery and work took her thoughts off of her sadness. When the baby whimpered she gazed up at an occasional cow grazing the hill and pretended Lacero was there, riding a fast horse.

Again in the night Grandmother came to point out cattails that could be pulled apart to make a soft, absorbent cushion for the baby's bottom.

One afternoon Esperanza brought home a piece of fine-woven cloth to dress the baby in, and frowned when Maria Inés appeared disinterested. "You son needs it," she insisted.

Maria Inés attempted to find the answer. "Surely it does not come from the sacred vestments."

Esperanza shook her head. "You think God will miss a little cloth? But, no, not from the church."

"From Señora Rios? Surely not. The woman has been kind to us."

"No."

"Then where? In all the Mission there is no cloth."

"This is true."

"Only the *bandidos* have such riches."

Esperanza smiled.

Maria Inés tried to keep her voice low, but her shock was great. "Who would steal from the thieves? We will be killed in our sleep! You must give it back."

Her friend shook her head so violently that her hair shook like the horses' tails. "Surely they stole it from a Mexican lady. You hear the stories *Sonoreños* tell about the trail. No one comes here from Mexico without losing their wealth—or their life. It is only right these evil men offer a gift for the baby."

"How do you be so bold?"

Esperanza's eyes blazed with excitement she had not shown

for many days. "While they were eating inside, I passed by their empty camp. It was in a saddlebag, easy to find."

Maria Inés imagined taking such a chance. "What else did you find?"

Esperanza held up a small sack of gold dust. "This was inside the cloth."

"No! It cannot be!" Maria Inés looked around to see if anyone was watching. "You must bury it. Let no one see what you have."

Esperanza looked pleased. "It is for your son. Maybe these men killed his father. Maybe they accuse each other of taking it and they shoot each other with their pistolas. Serve them right." She deposited the sack into Maria Inés's hand and laughed. "Let the Mexicanos see we are not helpless. They may think so, but we will survive even their cruel ways. Now go hide your son's gold."

"It will be his baptismal gift. The new padre will hold the service tomorrow. You will be the godmother."

It was Esperanza's turn to look surprised. "You do not ask Señora Rios? Her pride will suffer."

"We are no longer neophyte children. No one tells me who I choose. You are my choice." Maria Inés squeezed the sack of gold dust. "You will be godmother to my son. We need no one, only each other."

She waited until the moon was high before she hurried into the darkness where the first row of oaks formed a canopy a hundred feet from the church. Beneath the large oak where Grandmother had stood watching her people in the last hours before she joined them, Maria Inés dug a hole and buried the leather sack. It was a good tree. The same tree in which Padre Lasuen, Padre Serra's successor, hung the cross in dedication to San Miguel de Arcángel.

In the moon-shadow she carefully dug a hole and slipped her

sack inside before covering it up again and marking the spot with a large stone. When she was satisfied the place would pass undetected, she returned to the child who carried her husband's name.

Esperanza was waiting.

Maria Inés nodded. "It is done as you said." Even Esperanza would not know where the gold was hidden.

CHAPTER FIFTEEN

"I travel with you." Maria Inés balled her fists in fear and desperation, but she kept her voice low. "There is nothing left in the storehouses but the poles. Even old Padre Abella is dying. The Yanqui newcomers should take pity on him, sharing his small portion of jerked meat with the children. He lays most of the day on his stiff bed that creaks like his bones." She eased her fists and continued. "There is nothing left for us."

Esperanza shook her head. "You must return to Señora Rios. She has a large family to care for and she has been good to you."

Maria Inés tried not to allow the weight of responsibility sway her argument. "Her husband looks with desire on the Mission property. In time he may pay a little gold and he will own all the land. It does not seem right for Padre Cabot's life to be sold so cheaply."

"Padre Cabot's? What about ours? What did we get? Remember when the men come from Mexico and tell us the land is ours? They come, all saying the same thing. But what do we get—a bullet in the heart for your Lacero."

Maria Inés turned away to collect her thoughts. Esperanza was too quick to anger, and not always did she make the right choice, like now. "I will go with you to the ocean, to the ranchero of our friend, Rafael Villa. I want my son to learn the old ways."

Esperanza stood with the child in her arms. She spent as much time with Miguelito as his own mother, waiting for God to send her a child of her own. Maria Inés knew Esperanza could not leave the boy behind.

Esperanza knew it as well. "What if there is no work for you? It will be better for you to stay here where you are known. We will take Miguelito with us. You can come later, after the rains. We will have a place ready for you."

Maria Inés felt the blood leaving her face. Give up the child, even for a while?

"Think of the boys killed by the Yanquis. You cannot keep him safe. He needs a man to look out for him. Lacero would agree if he were here."

"You do not know this!" Maria Inés did not allow herself to show weakness.

Jose Toma, who had been standing in the shadows, spoke up. "She speaks true. Your husband would not want his son to be in danger. He would want him to go to the Villa Rancho and become a great vaquero."

Both of them against her? Even Señora, when she heard of the plan, would agree with them. Maria Inés turned and left the room intending to walk into the night where she could think. Instead, a group of travelers was arriving who needed to be fed. Always she was summoned to work while others rested—why should tonight be any different? Maybe Esperanza was right and God intended her to stay behind and make other people's lives easier, a sacrifice for her son's safety. If Lacero had lived they would be safely at Mission San Antonio, but in a moment of weakness after his death she had returned to San Miguel and now she had no way to provide for her son. Perhaps it was God's will she suffer. With a sigh, she turned her steps in the direction of the church to watch Padre greet the carretas arriving.

"Did you have a safe journey?" the padre asked, as he did of each new arrival.

"Banditos on the trail." The man was agitated, his tone resigned. "They took the silver we brought with us intending to purchase land. Everything is gone. Everything."

Padre sighed. It was the same tale told more nights than not; and yet the Sonoreños continued to arrive from northern Mexico in their straggling caravans spread out too sparsely for adequate defense. "I am sorry. With God's grace you suffered no injuries?"

"Even there the truth will grieve you. The diablos took the life of one of our most trusted men, first robbing him of his worldly goods and then torturing him most heinously."

A common tale as well. The padre shifted his weight as if it took all of his strength to stand. Maria stood quietly so as not to interfere with the conversation, and so she could hear what was said.

"Stripped the man naked before the entire caravan. They gouged out his eyes with the tip of a knife—for sport! And made him walk toward the ravine as a warning to the rest of us. We watched him stagger and lose his way among the bushes until he fell to his death on the rocks. It was a death such as I never wish to think of again."

"You buried him there?"

The man looked up, haunted. "They prevented it. We were herded forward like sheep shorn of our coats. Grateful to escape the same fate."

For a moment Padre was silent. Maria Inés had time to think about her friend's words, *You cannot keep him safe.* Maybe she was right; she and Jose Toma, both right.

The man was still talking as his spent, exhausted family climbed out of the wagons. "The government is happy to have us sacrifice to keep this land from the Americanos' control. It is a political game to them, nothing more."

Padre motioned with a shaking finger to his lips. "Many

travelers stop here at night. Some are Californios, hoping for a suitable treaty with the Americans, some are Mexicanos, satisfied with the strong rule we now have. The lines are drawn. You must use caution if you do not want to find yourself imprisoned for treason. Many young men have found themselves exactly so."

The Mexican retracted, his face haggard and weary. "I have had enough of politics and sparring. I only want to find a few acres where I can raise cattle and provide for my family."

Padre nodded. "Perhaps you should inquire of Señor Rios. He may be interested in making an arrangement."

The man shook his head. "This land does not support enough cattle. And besides, thanks to those cutthroats, I have no money. I have heard, up north, Señor Vallejo has been generous in giving his land away. He has fought in the Mexican courts to save his claim on the land. But he is unable to prove his ownership and since it is clear he will not prevail he is generously giving his land to those whom the courts will smile upon."

"Insanity. The very thing Mexico rebelled against with their Spanish yoke, she is decreeing onto her own citizens. Señor Vallejo's only crime is that he is Spanish, not Mexican. For *that* he has been ruined."

"And yet I am Mexican, ruined by wild Indians who held us up on the road."

Padre shook his head, his voice weak with exhaustion. "Not wild Indians. Our tribes do not accost, but steal in secret when there is no one to notice. You have been robbed by a band of cholos, mongrels who have taken their feelings of betrayal out on anyone within reach. They are not Indians, but half-breeds. They are joined by sailors, and deserters who jumped ship because stealing is easier than honest work."

The man's eyes were haunted by the memory of what he had seen.

"As for the other," Padre hesitated, "I fear your description of diablo is accurate. Like all devils, they find pleasure in giving pain."

The man stood, looking dazed and uncertain, as though he would soon drop of exhaustion. Padre allowed him to accompany him to his quarters, undoubtedly to offer him the last dreg of brandy remaining.

At Mass the next day, a visiting priest presided. He had not come to say service for the handful of people in the church. Instead, he had come to take Padre Abella to Mission Santa Ynez, to die among his beloved hollyhocks. "I am sorry. There is no money to support a priest here anymore. You must try to stay together and pray. We can do nothing more for you. *Vaya con Dios.*"

Maria Inés clasped her son to her side as he strained to crawl on the floor to the other boys. She watched the way he struggled against her control and she understood even though he was a child, he already had a vision for his life she could not share. Perhaps Toma and Esperanza were blessed by God, for they prospered while she suffered only loss. Her son would be safer with them. And she could not leave Padre to suffer his indignities alone.

When Mass ended, Jose Toma and Esperanza approached her and stood quietly while Esperanza cast quick glances at Miguelito, squirming in his mother's arms. When the child reached for his godmother it seemed as though he made the decision for himself. With grieving heart Maria Inés handed over the child and watched as he batted a small fist at Jose Toma's nose. Her friends did not meet her eyes and she knew it was because there was nothing more to be said.

At the time of departure, she stood in the shade of the church and watched the small group begin their journey. Jose Toma carried Miguelito on his shoulders, but no one spoke. The silence carried her through a moment of weakness when she longed to clutch him to her bosom and run with him to the river to hide. She watched without tears until her son disappeared on the same road that had claimed his father. He would be safe because each day she would work hard and her labors would be a sacrifice for his safety. Each day, also, she would kneel on the hard tile of the church and offer prayers that the banditos would not find them.

Her thoughts occupied her until the three were only small dots in the distance. Then she turned back toward her duties and worked until her pain turned to dullness.

The feeling of deadness continued as she served the padres a meager lunch before they left to travel to Santa Ynez. She tried to concentrate on their conversation so she would understand why such bad things were happening to her people.

The visiting priest spoke between bites of tortilla. "They say Governor Pico means to sell off the Missions."

"Bah. He is a man whose character is too small for the office he holds." Padre Abella's voice was weak with sorrow and weariness. "He was a seller of spirits before he was made governor. Spirits served in horn vessels with false bottoms . . ."

Maria Inés turned to hide her smile.

". . . but the sale of these lands is prohibited by the government. I have read the papers, myself."

"It makes no matter. He intends to do it quickly, to his friends and those he owes favors. They say he needs money to fight his political campaigns."

Padre Abella clasped his hands, fingers in a prayerful position, a piece of tortilla between his thin fingers. "Please God to help us, I will pray it is not so."

"Already he has sold San Luis Obispo de Tolosa. There are petitions for this one already on his desk."

Maria Inés bit her lip as she removed the plates from the

table. Her hands shook and she didn't meet the gaze of the men, but held her head high with pride that she had been chosen to serve this last meal. When Padre Abella climbed into his carreta to begin the long trip to Santa Ynez, she stood like a statue, not moving until the cart—and the accompanying padre and his guard—disappeared down El Camino Real heading south. Only then did she turn and make her way to the river, to weep among the willows.

When evening came, she returned to find the grounds as silent as a tomb. Without the priest the other Indians seemed as lost as she. Someone brought out clay dice and began a half-hearted game, but there was nothing left to gamble and the men showed little interest. She looked up and saw the clay tiles on the roof her father had made before she was born. Inside her room was the metate her mother had used to grind corn, hidden from the women who would have taken it for their own use as they had taken everything else. The courtyard had been stripped bare. Some of the local families had taken things for safekeeping, like the Wishing Chair, in the hopes that one day the Mission would be healed. But for now its bones had been broken.

Many of her people slept beneath the portico that night, as though they needed to be together. In the morning they stood in a group waiting—for what?

Dawn had just begun to slide past the night when Maria Inés rose to return to the Rios adobe, her heart as dry as the patches of turkey grass scenting the air.

From the top of the hill an army of mounted men spilled over the hills of golden grass with silent precision—men in numbers many times greater than the men and women who remained behind at the Mission. Maria Inés watched as the leader signaled for his men to halt. He took from his saddlebag a brass tube and used it to sweep his gaze across the Mission compound. She could sense his fierce determination. Even though she had never seen the uniform the man wore, she knew from where they had come—and why. They were no warring Indian tribe, not even Mexicans. They were the American band of riffraff, soldiers, hired mountain men, and ruffians that had been making a slow, meandering path from Mission San Antonio, trying to keep their animals alive on the sparse grass. A runner had arrived days earlier with the news. The word had gone out to the neighboring ranchos and the men were ready to defend the Mission. But they had not expected so many.

"Yanquis," she whispered. "It is the one they call Path-Finder. They will steal everything like they did at Monterey. I must warn Padre." She took several steps before she remembered the padre had disappeared in the distance. But war was not the padre's business, even if he had been still here. As she scuttled out of the way, a trio of caballeros from nearby ranchos loyal to Mexico stumbled out of the barracks. Overhead, the flag of Mexico waved proudly in the chill December air.

A few soldados with no better place to go were already mounting a ragged defense when two men from the hillside split off from the group and advanced, one carrying a white flag, the other an American flag folded across his lap. The two Yanquis rode bravely into the courtyard and halted. By then a handful of men had gathered to hear what they had to say. The important-looking Yanqui spoke loudly, scarcely waiting for the Indian to translate into Spanish.

"You are standing on American territory. You will immediately surrender your flag and submit to the authority of the United States or face the consequences."

One of the soldados who had designated himself the leader, stroked his face as if deciding what he should do. "We will need to discuss our decision, Señor. *Excuse, por favor.*" He turned and led the men out of the hearing. After many minutes the small band of Mexicans returned. The soldado leader puffed his chest and declared, "We have decided, Señor. Tell your commadante we are fully garrisoned and we will not surrender to your authority. Not until one man remains alive will we betray our flag."

The two Yanquis turned and rode back to their waiting commander.

From a corner of the courtyard six Indians were struggling with heavy leather sacks, probably gold and silver from the cattle hide trade the padres had left behind because the authorities would confiscate it if they found it and the money belonged to the Indians. The six disappeared into a small house at the corner of the courtyard. She heard the sound of digging and while the garrison watched the Yanquis on the hill, the Indians returned carrying their shovels and spades. A while later one of them emerged carrying a heavy branch the gardeners used for sweeping the dirt. Then they retreated back into the Mission.

From the hill a cannon roar blasted the silence. Maria Inés cowered with her hands over her head when an explosion ripped through the air. She looked up in time to see a piece of adobe wall explode into the courtyard. Overhead, the Mexican flag was being quickly lowered to the ground. A moment later the flagpole was empty.

The hillside exploded with movement. She turned to see where she might hide, but the others were milling around as uncertain as she, none of them wanting to miss the excitement. One of the soldados called out, "Four hundred Yanqui devils. Mother of God, save us."

The troops marched onto the grounds, followed by many carretas drawn by fat oxen that she recognized as belonging to a hacienda to the north. Many of the cattle and bullocks had also come from the haciendas, for they did not have the haggard look of the Yanquis' horses. The commander introduced himself as Señor Fremont. Maria Inés studied his face and did not see a reckless nature in his manners or appearance, so she remained in the shadow of the portico and watched. The commander seemed surprised to find only twenty armed Mexicans standing at attention, prepared to surrender. He issued a command and his men searched the rooms in case more men were hiding, but they found none.

The Mexican soldado sounded fierce as he stood proudly at attention in his stiff uniform and announced, "Señor, we live to fight another day. Next time, we will meet as equals and the advantage will be ours." Maria Inés recalled the many times the soldados had harassed the neophytes, acting proud and arrogant, even today vowing to defend the compound with their lives and then, minutes later, surrendering after only one shot fired. They were like fierce dogs, outnumbered and taking refuge against the master's leg so that they would not be harmed. But even she understood there was nothing to be done, twenty against many hundreds.

Afterwards, the Yanquis raised their own flag onto the flagpole and they butchered thirteen cattle and invited the Mexicans to join them for a celebration. The Yanquis had liquor and the talk grew jovial as the night drew on. By morning the caballeros rode out for their ranchos. They were allowed to keep their weapons to protect themselves from the bandidos roaming the roads, with the promise they would return to their wives and seek a peaceful life.

Señor Fremont and his men departed, two days later, with saddlebags filled with whatever they could plunder. Maria Inés wandered over to the small house where the gold was said to be hidden. The door had been blocked. Inside, the dirt floor had been swept clean with brush marks. She watched, but she never saw any of the Indians return to the house. It was the way of the white men that the Indians would never see the gold if the padres had indeed left it for them.

But she had a secret. Across the yard, under the trees, her small sack of gold was still waiting.

Chapter Sixteen

Maria Inés paused on her way to retrieve Señora's silver hair combs. The woman's waist-length hair was scrubbed and ready for plaiting. Each week the task took the better part of a morning and today was no different. Washing hair was not hard work, only another of the daily chores. She was satisfied enough with the work, but not a day went by she did not think about Miguelito. Ten years had passed since she last saw him, ten years of prayers and sacrifice for his safety.

Unlike herself, Señora Rios had received God's blessings. She possessed airs of refinement, learned during her previous life among the gente de razón in Monterey. This, along with her love of God, gave her a happy heart. She possessed a hearty disposition that made childbearing easy and God had blessed her with many children.

The Rios family enjoyed a new home, a large and light one-story hacienda on the Estrella River with four heavy doors providing security in the event of an attack, even if it left the interior gloomy in the cold months.

The abandoned Mission San Miguel remained without a priest, the private quarters vacant. Señor Rios had petitioned the government for the deed to the lands, but he had heard nothing. The air at Señor Rios's estate, on the east side of the Salinas River, was clearer than on the west side, and it was away from El Camino Real, therefore safer from strangers for a family with many small children, but the rancho was three leagues from the Mission and she missed seeing the church.

Señor Rios was a kind employer, direct in manner and sure of his position as befitted a man of his experience. He had been a sergeant of the escolte and she recalled him as a fair man before he left to accept a promotion in Monterey. He married while he was away, and returned with a wife and three children. Since that time they had added several more to their family.

Today he was in his office, speaking to two men.

"Governor Pico has passed a decree allowing our petition to be considered. Consider these words as I read them. 'There will be sold at this capital, to the highest bidder, the Mission of San Miguel . . . among others.' " He glanced up, but fortunately he did not see her standing at the door. "There is more. Listen. 'If the neophytes do not return to Mission San Miguel within the month, it will be declared without owners and subject to sale.' "

Another gentleman, whom she recognized as the Englishman, Señor Piloto Reed, laughed. "Why the greedy old buzzard. He means to do it!"

Señor Jose Garcia, a handsome Mexican who had been a friend of the Rios family for many years, spoke with excitement in his voice. "It is the perfect opportunity. Let us submit a request for the properties. The buildings are vacant, and some are still habitable. The land is sufficient to raise cattle and crops."

"How much should we petition for?" Piloto Reed asked.

"The lands remaining are twelve square leagues, *mas o menos* a league or two as is the custom." As Señor Rios spoke he pulled out a sheet of parchment and quill, and began to write. "We will each put up three hundred dollars."

Señor Garcia's face paled. "It will take a while for me to obtain the funds."

Señor Rios scarcely looked up. "We will offer six hundred. It is enough for this dry land that is so hot in the summer. Good for nothing but sheep." He glanced out the window, his face filled with satisfaction. "I will apply for a permit to serve liquor to all of the travelers who pass along our roads. They will need somewhere to rest after a hard day's ride. We will feed and water their horses. I will appoint a majordomo to run the place in my absence."

Maria Inés froze, her hands leaden so that the combs fell to the floor. She knelt to pick them up, glad her hair covered her burning face. The neophytes had mostly disappeared from the Mission—most of them were hiding along the river where they would be safer from the whites. She had visited in previous months and found only thirty remaining, poor and starved, the children sick and listless, but now even those were gone. She had brought a basket filled with dried and fresh meat and vegetables, gifts from the Señora. Now the Mission was abandoned and the Indian people would lose their rights. Who could she tell? There was no one. Without a horse she could not ride to San Antonio, where many of her people still resided, and warn them they needed to return to claim what was theirs.

Feigning calmness she didn't feel, she returned to complete Senora's hair, making one-word responses to the woman's chatter until she would escape into the kitchen without betraying the turmoil raging inside her.

All week she kept an eye out for someone who might help her, but the only strangers who stopped were hard-looking men who did not seem sympathetic to the plight of a poor Indian. Instead, they looked so fearsome that she kept her eyes down as she sold them provisions for their journey.

Each night she tossed on her mat, unable to sleep because her heart was heavy with guilt. She remembered her girlhood and the fiestas and High Masses, the lovely voices of the choir, the great carcasses of beef roasted on a spit over the coals, each person eating their fill along with tortillas, frijoles, pie, and vegetables. At night on her mat on the kitchen floor, the scent of lemons filled her senses—and olives as they were being crushed into oil for cooking. A thousand memories flooded back, even the stifling nights in the monjério, but her heart was too heavy for tears. It was good her mother had taught her Indian girls do not cry. If she had known how, she would be dried up by now.

Within a month Señor Rios received an important letter. He and Piloto Reed read its contents while they drank wine, and afterwards slapped each other on the backs. Maria Inés served the beverage and tried to keep her hands steady as the celebration extended to include their wives and children.

"Guillermo says we are to move into the priests' quarters. It will seem strange at first, but I believe we will be comfortable there."

Señora Reed was Indian, from a northern tribe. It was said she was the illegitimate daughter of Mariano Guadalupe Vallejo, the great Don Vallejo's brother. They were nice people, although Piloto Reed was more talkative and trusting of his fellow countrymen than a native-born Californio would be.

"For some reason," Señor Rios said, "My friend Señor Garcia has chosen to distance himself from me. With the gift of a few horses and other valuables he was glad to pursue other interests. It seems his heart was not in the enterprise, although as a Mexican, his nationality played a role in our obtaining the land." His voice held a lilt of humor as he glanced over at his fair-haired partner. He obviously enjoyed this rare occasion to have the better of the Yanquis, no matter how congenial his partner might be. Maria Inés set the tray of beverages on the table and turned without betraying the direction of her thoughts.

"That makes you the controlling partner?" Señor Reed asked in a worried tone.

Señor Rios dismissed his concerns with a wave of his hand. "We will each have the right to buy out the other's interests if we choose."

"And if one of us should die?"

"In the unlikely event the entire family should perish then the rights would revert to the surviving partner. Otherwise we would be expected to be gallant and buy the widow out for a fair and reasonable sum."

Maria Inés turned to leave the room, careful she did not shut the door in a manner that would draw attention to herself. *Fair and reasonable?* Only three modest tracts of poor land, Las Gallinas, El Nacimiento, and La Estrella left to the Indians? Each held in trust by the church, and none large enough to provide a living for so many people. But what did a Mexican governor care about fairness? The leaders changed as often as Señora Rios washed her hair. The people did not want those worthless pieces of land. They had petitioned to have the lands they loved returned to them—El Paso de Robles or La Asunción, the heart of the homeland where the soil was better and hunting was still possible.

She returned to the kitchen and began plucking hens for the noon meal with short, angry strokes until four hens lay naked and ready for roasting. With so many mouths to feed she was too busy to think—a good thing. It was her son's birthday. He was twelve today. A man.

Outside, the children were playing a kicking game with their ball. Señora Rios had more children than she could count, each one living under her roof, but Maria Inés had only one and she had not seen her son in many years. Her heart ached with the need to know if he was growing up tall and proud like his father. Soon he would be grown and her sacrifice for his safety would be over. She turned and watched the oldest boy kicking the ball. Jose Camilo Guadalupe Rios, born the same year of her own son, every movement the boy made—a reminder.

The meal was served outdoors where gentle west breezes

from the river cooled the land. Señora Rios charmed her visitors with stories of growing up in Monterey. Between sips of lemonade she told of foreign visitors who arrived at the Custom House to pay their tariffs and arrange for trade with the residents, and proud Californio men who took sides in the military coups occurring between rival factions. She even described the exploits of Dona Ana Maria Gonzales and her friend, Dona Cruz, the supposed niece of Governor Chico, who was, in fact, his mistress. According to Señora Rios, the actions of these beautiful and scandalous women caused frequent upsets among the gente de razón.

Maria Inés had never heard a woman speak so boldly, but Señora's stories were shared with her kinsman. Señor Reed's wife was her niece, if only an illegitimate one, and an Indian at that, but Señora Reed was happy to have a woman to visit with. Señor Reed's mother-in-law assisted with the couple's two-year-old son who was quiet and shy.

The men did not speak of business for the rest of the afternoon, only to agree Señor Reed and his family would have the padres' rooms at the Mission as their living quarters. Although they did not mention it, Maria Inés had overheard them talking about another petition denied Señor Rios. He had not told his wife yet, but the family would have to leave this comfortable home to take up residence in the two-story adobe near the Mission where travelers—and bandidos—could stop at any time of the day to barter for provisions. The Señora would not be happy with the move, for it put her children at risk when her husband was away.

By the time the families had bedded down for the night, Maria Inés's bare feet felt like they were on fire. A starving Indian craftsman had stopped by just the day before and measured the children for shoes. He was drilling and sewing them somewhere out in the brush and had promised to return with the completed boots within a week. Perhaps he would make a pair of sandals to replace her own, worn through. Señora Rios might agree to pay for them in exchange for a few months' work.

The next morning Señora Rios asked Maria Inés to accompany the Reeds to help settle them into their rooms at the Mission.

She walked beside the slow-moving oxen because there was no room inside the carreta, hurrying ahead to catch a glimpse of her former home. The Mission was not as dead as she had feared. Pigeons and doves roosted beneath the tiles, busy with their nests and their feeding. Rabbits hopped through the tiled arcade nibbling shoots of grass between the cobblestones. But she saw no Indians milling around, only the ghosts of a past glory.

Once the boxes were unloaded and carried to their rooms, it seemed strange to see another family occupying Padre Cabot's quarters. She smoothed Piloto Reed's blue wool coat and hung it on a hook that had once held Padre's worn habit. The coat was very grand, with gold piping and brass buttons, his uniform left over from the years when he served as a sea pilot on the trading ships. For this reason everyone called him Piloto. She didn't think he minded.

Piloto was polite and respectful when he asked her advice. "Maria Inés, do you know a woman who would be willing to live here and help with the household? We have a Negress cook coming from Monterey later this month."

"No, Señor. They are all gone. Maybe a woman will return once she hears a family's laughter once again."

He nodded and returned to unloading his wagon. She looked longingly at the rags Señora Reed pulled from a bundle to scrub the dust with.

Maria Inés took a breath and dared to speak. "A broom made from soap bush would clean the corners better."

171

The Señora smiled and held the scrap of cloth for her to take. "I would wish for such a broom. Perhaps in time. My husband brings many sheep to the land. He has purchased a spinning wheel for me to use. I will need a room to put it, and the loom."

"You are blessed. I will show you the room where you should work. The light is good there—windows made with scraped sheep belly. My father made them."

The door to the room was swollen with moisture and disuse, but she pushed hard and it opened with a squeal of stiff leather hinges. Inside, the room held the smell of work. For a moment it seemed like a day out of the past, even more so when Señor Reed carried the spinning wheel inside and set it near the window. He soon returned with pieces of the loom that would need to be reconstructed when he had time. Maria Inés closed her eyes and ran her fingers along the smooth wood, hearing the *thwack-thwack* of the shuttle in the hands of the Indian girls. "Hemp makes a strong warp if you can find it. Better than wool." The words were hard to speak and she stopped after just a few.

Señora Reed looked up and her eyes said she understood. "You have lost so much. My people, too. I am fortunate to have married a good man. You will, too."

Maria Inés kept her face expressionless. No one here knew the story of Lacero's death. She had spoken of it in the past with Señora Rios, although she had kept the secret of her child to herself. The woman meant no disrespect in mentioning a new husband. She was only offering hope for a future.

Maria Inés turned to lead the way outside where the air seemed easier. "I pray you find a woman to help you, Señora."

CHAPTER SEVENTEEN

Maria Inés set her mind to the idea of leaving for the Villa Rancho before the summer heat. Already the days were growing in intensity and the journey would take a month. She planned to announce her plan as soon as Señora Rios finished feeding her big brood of children and set them to play outside. But before she could find the words, the Señora announced news of her own.

"My husband leaves for the goldfields tomorrow. He and Señor Reed will be away for the spring and summer. They mean to drive a herd of sheep to sell to the miners. They say fresh meat is more valuable than gold dust." She looked worried, even though her words were brave. "This year's rains were not sufficient for the sheep. The grass is sparse and the coyotes are eating well. We must have gold for taxes."

Maria Inés understood the words not said: *I will need you now, more than ever.* But the woman would not say the words to a servant, even if they were true.

"When you finish with the dishes, we will need the table to clean beans today. I will put the older girls to the task. My son can read the catechism as we work."

Maria Inés worked quietly, listening to the young man, his head bent over the book, his fingers tracing the path of the words, and her heart longed to see her son. *Perhaps when the men return with a full sack of gold.* She turned so the boy's profile didn't tear at her memory as she began her next task.

★ ★ ★ ★ ★

The summer season seemed long while they waited for word from the goldfields. Maria Inés spent hours hoeing and watering vegetables that supplemented the endless diet of mutton. The children complained, but she was grateful hunger no longer growled inside her. Sometimes strangers stopped to buy a sack of horsebeans and a chunk of mutton for their campfires, and they told about the dangers and the hardships of the gold camps. Many of them had been robbed and had scarcely enough money to buy their meal, but each understood that no one had enough wealth to offer the food for free. The sight of so many children playing in the yard or doing chores reminded the travelers that they were lucky to have only themselves to provide for. This is what Maria Inés told herself each time a skinny, ragged Indian waited in the sagebrush for her to carry them a bowl of beans.

Each night Señora Rios required her children kneel in the kitchen and say a rosary for their father's safe return. Maria Inés added her own special intentions.

Señora was kind to let her sleep in the kitchen on her *tule* mat. In the winter months and in the heat of the afternoons, she sat at the table and wove baskets from the *tule* reeds she found at the river, the basket bottoms woven so tight they held water. She added bits of shells for ornamentation so they would sell better. Sometimes, when Señora finished putting her children to bed, she would bring her mending and the two of them would work together silently.

Grandmother no longer came to her in her dreams. Neither did Lacero anymore. In her dreams, waking and sleeping, she was an island.

In late fall, when the oaks began dropping their acorns, one day was different from the others. The children began shouting and crying to their mother to come quickly. From the doorway

Maria Inés watched as two horses raced into the yard. From one, a haggard man dismounted and bent to hug his son. Soon each of the children demanded their turn and then it was Señora's turn to be embraced in front of everyone. Señor Rios was in a fine mood, tired and thin, but happy to be home. Maria Inés retreated into the cook room and set another plate on the table.

After expressing his courtesies, Piloto Reed rode past, bound for his own family. A happy family reunion would occur tonight.

The gold that was to be their salvation was contained in small pouches like the one Maria Inés had buried under the tree. Señor was pleased with his earnings, a pouch of gold he claimed weighed five pounds. He allowed each child to hold the leather pouch before he handed it to his wife for burying when everyone was asleep. He laughed because the youngest could scarcely lift the bag.

His stories kept the children awake until past their bedtimes, and still he talked, laughing and gesturing, making the room seem larger. Maria Inés quietly finished her dishes and moved to the veranda where the stars called to her from the clear, dark sky. A voice carried on the wind, blowing from the coast, telling her it was time. She listened to the way the trees carried the message closer and closer, ensuring that she heard.

By the time the children settled down, and the couple secured the heavy doors and windows and made their way upstairs, she returned inside to make preparations for sleeping on her mat.

In the morning Señora Rios was all smiles. A family restored. She announced that her husband wanted to take a trip farther south to see his land holdings.

"You will accompany us, of course. The children are fond of you." She clapped her hands in enthusiasm. "We are traveling to see where we may live one day. Come. We must pack for several days."

Maria Inés felt her stomach churning. Now was the time to explain her plan to return to her son. Now, before the Señora announced she was carrying another baby or that the Señor was leaving for another adventure. But instead of speaking, she slowly nodded and returned to the pot of beans she was stirring.

The family packing was not hard. In no time the carreta was filled with pots and pans cushioned in bedding between heavy sacks of meat and dried beans. The children rode in a second carreta behind the first one Piloto Reed loaned them for the trip. Señora Reed stood by with her small son, waving goodbye. She was carrying another child inside her and she could not lift heavy things.

The autumn sun offered a warm day for the trip. The children were boisterous and in an adventurous mood as they bounced about in the cart pulled by a pair of oxen. Once again Maria Inés turned and watched the Mission disappear behind her, its red tiles the last thing she saw as the oxen lumbered south.

The small caravan continued for two hours without stopping until they reached the site Señor Rios planned for their new home. When the children asked for food, Maria Inés spread a leather hide on the ground and ladled frijoles into tortillas for the children. The oldest son, Jose Camilo, was not among them. He had ridden ahead with his father, a proud young man with square, high shoulders already formed to the yoke of privilege. She found it hard when it was necessary to speak to him. Instead of gazing directly at him, she found something to do with her hands as an excuse so she would not have to look at his eyes. Everything in his manner annoyed her and she knew she was hard on him because she harbored resentment. Many times she prayed for a priest to hear her confession over the matter.

Señor Rios was a prosperous man who always had an eye to his wealth. He hoped his petition for La Estrella would be approved. He had filed it just before the Americans claimed the territory as their own and he was unsure whether his rights would be considered. Maria Inés had heard whisperings about the misfortunes of the Rios family, suffered under the Americans, and the indignity that he had to resort to their courts to uphold his rights. He had been an important man to the Mexicans, but no longer so to the Americans.

Piloto Reed likewise feared for his property. He had received a letter saying he would have to share the Mission with a priest when one could be spared for the small parish of San Miguel. Señora Reed would probably like having Mass again and she would not mind sharing her home, but Piloto was an Englishman and he needed to *own* the land. As did Señor Rios.

Maria Inés held her anger inside. The Señora exaggerated when she said the children needed a poor Indian servant; the children only needed their mother to tell stories of her childhood. Each day of the holiday outing was a success, but it rekindled memories she could no longer contain. They returned home on the third day, and as she retraced her steps to La Estrella behind the lumbering carretas, Maria Inés made her plans.

On the fifth morning in December, when breakfast chores were completed, she packed her things into her burden basket and started her journey. She was too shamed to speak to the Señora, so she said nothing and simply melted into the sagebrush while the children were down for their naps.

By sunset she reached the Mission. The chill afternoon air had sent everyone indoors where a fire was burning in the cook stove. Maria Inés looked with envy at the heavy door separating the cold day from the comfort she would find inside. She started toward the room, but hesitated lest Señora Reed would send her back. The door opened and she saw a group of rough-looking men warming themselves at the cooking fire. A moment later Señora Reed left the room as she often did when strange men stopped for the night. It was her husband's rule.

The Señora was big with child. Her young brother, Señor Jose Vallejo, was living with them until his mother arrived to care for the family. It was obvious Señora Reed was ready to deliver, for her husband had obtained the services of Señora Olivera, the midwife. The midwife's daughter was with them, carrying her young son on her hip as the three women walked the arcade to their rooms. The little Reed boy skipped ahead, happy to be free of his mother's hand because he was now a big boy of four. Maria Inés smiled and kept her eyes on the handsome young child.

The women and children disappeared into their rooms and soon the small windows in the barred doors flickered with light from the newly lit candles. Maria Inés shivered as the sun slipped over the hill in the waning heat of the early December day. It would be an easy matter to knock on their door and seek shelter for the night—and yet something held her back. Perhaps it was the thought of sleeping in the Padre's quarters. Even after two years it still seemed strange to have the Reed family take such liberties.

She slipped her burden basket from her shoulders and placed her *tule* mat underneath her for warmth. She would sleep in the neophyte quarters where she and her husband had once lived. She would wait there until dark and slip out, careful no one saw her steal over to the line of trees where she had buried her gold. Before the moon crested the hill behind her she would use a sharp stone to dig a hole in the sand.

A moment later, she heard a door open and saw one of the men leave the cook room and walk to the wood pile beneath the covered veranda and begin loading his arms with small pieces of wood. He was a tall man with sharp features and the shifty-eyed look of a thief. With his arms full he hesitated, then picked up the ax that Señor Piloto used when he chopped the wood.

With a furtive glance around, the man returned to the cook room.

From a distance the old sheepherder who had tended the Padre's flocks was coming home from the fields with his grandchild, both wrapped in pelts to ward off the cold. Maria Inés thought about the new basket she had finished. The man might be glad to trade for such a pelt. Perhaps tomorrow, when the old Indian had eaten and rested for the night, she would approach him.

She watched as the two paused at the cook room door and entered. A moment later they returned with steaming bowls of frijoles and mutton. She could taste the meal on her lips, the memory of Padre's atole filling her with longing.

The Mission was quiet again. Maria Inés made a move to rise and seek shelter when a sudden squawk, like a bird in distress, came from inside the cookhouse.

Suddenly the door flew open and six men ran out, one carrying the ax, another carrying a pistola, and a third, a cutlass like the soldados wore. In the shadow of the arcade she could not see their faces, but they ran crouched along the corridor like soldiers. Three of them burst into the rooms Señora Reed and the other women occupied. The others ran in the direction the sheepherder and his grandson had gone. Maria Inés looked around, frantic to find Piloto Reed, but he was not to be seen. Then she remembered he had been in the cook room and a shiver of fear ran down her spine.

Soon women's screams filled the air, punctuated by the sound of children crying. Maria Inés waited, her hand clenched over her mouth to keep from crying out. From the rear of the building some of the men were returning. The screams and groans were quiet now, the only sounds the loud cries and commands of men gone mad with murder. On the arcade a body lay where it had fallen, but the men stepped around it as if it were a log.

Maria was quaking like a willow, but she was too afraid to move. She crouched low and brought her knees into her belly so that she melted into the shadows. She controlled her fear so the men would not smell it, like grizzlies could smell the fear of the hunter.

The men returned to the room where Señora Reed's limp body was slumped over the bed. They entered and soon departed, carrying a woman by her legs and arms, her dress dragging on the cobblestones as they hurried to the carpenter's shop. Two more men brought out the midwife in a similar fashion, and in another trip, her daughter. When these were disposed of they returned for the small bodies and carried them into the same room. The bodies were stacked like cordwood. As if this was not enough, they stacked wood on top and started a fire before they backed out and closed the door behind them.

The men returned to the women's quarters, the room once inhabited by Padre Cabot. In the flickering light Maria Inés watched their shadows dancing on the wall as they drank from a keg of wine and celebrated their deeds. When they had consumed their fill they took the ax and split open the chests where Señora Reed kept her lovely dresses and jewels. Laughing as though the murder of small children was a fiesta, they dumped the chests on the floor and divided the spoils.

A half hour passed in such madness. When they finished they strolled to their horses, laughing and gesturing like the diablos they were. They mounted with little regard for the animals. When they rode off toward the south, some of them passed near enough that she could have thrown a stone at them. One was wearing Señor Piloto's blue coat. Another was an Indian, his face impassive. The leader held a heavy bag jingling with coins. Each man held in his hands stockings or kerchiefs filled with things that did not belong to them; jewels not needed by the Señora anymore, either.

They reined their horses around, and for a moment it seemed they were going toward the Rios adobe. Maria Inés's stomach clenched with fear for the family. Instead they headed south, toward the village of San Luis Obispo de Tolosa.

They were only a short distance off when the leader threw down his heavy sack and shouted for the others to take their share. The others dismounted and scrambled to fill their stockings with silver. After a bit they remounted and started off again, this time at a run.

Maria Inés crouched in the sand, terrified to move for fear they would return. Cold bit into her chest and she drew her knees up tighter, willing herself to stay alert for any sound. In the morning the sound of horse hooves drew her from a dazed state of half-sleep filled with visions of blood and gore. She peered through the overhanging branches and saw two men approaching from the north. One she recognized as Señor Price, the *alcalde* of San Luis Obispo. The other was a stranger.

They waited for someone to come out and take their horses, and when moments passed and no one appeared, they dismounted, commenting about the absence of Señor Reed as they did so. A moment later she heard their shout of surprise as they traced the route of the murderers along the colonnade to where the women and children had been slain. At the discovery of a pool of blood, they grew quiet. They approached the half-open door of Señora Reed's room and stood shoulder-to-shoulder at the door, neither pushing forward to enter. Señor Price gagged and turned to void his stomach into the sand. The other man was barely inside before he was joined by Señor Price again, neither man uttering a word as they searched for bodies among the blood extending even under the bed.

Maria Inés waited for them to emerge. She wanted to stand and tell them where the children could be found, but her legs would not permit it. Still without speaking, the men followed the tracks of blood to the carpenter's workshop and opened the door. In her shock she had forgotten the fire. It had apparently burned itself out, for she heard the agonized shouts of the men when they discovered the bodies. When they returned they were staggering, seemingly blinded with horror. One made the sign of the cross over himself and she saw they both wept. The wind picked up and still they searched, the only sound, the tap of their boots on the cobblestones and the closing of doors. When they came to the cook room they slowly entered. After a few minutes they returned into the sunlight and mounted their horses to gallop toward the south.

She sat unmoving and tried to decide what she should do. She was so weary. She would wait beneath the tree until sunset and start south.

A few hours passed with only the ominous silence of the courtyard and a faint breeze that drove the cold into her lungs. The thundering hooves of a horse caused her to flatten herself against the ground again. A bear of a man, a Negro dressed in buckskin, rode up with the saddlebags of the mail courier behind his saddle—Señor Beckwourth, the mail courier. He swung from his horse and tied it at the railing before entering the common room to get a cup of hot coffee. Maria Inés watched, too paralyzed to call out to him. But her warning was not necessary—the gruesome scene lay before him.

At the door he saw the dark circle on the arcade and he advanced until his boots touched the pool of blood made by the ax. He returned to the half-opened door of the common room, entered quickly, and retreated. He kept his hand on the door as though he meant to close it, but stood instead like a statue as he looked around, listening for sounds. Then he seemed to sense he was not alone. He drew his pistola and started down the arcade, carefully opening each door. At the door where Señora Reed and her family had been murdered, he hesitated for long moments before he backed from the room. From across the courtyard Maria Inés saw the shudder consuming his big frame. He grasped his pistola and he, too, followed the trail of blood to the carpenter shop. When he saw what awaited him he turned and ran back to his horse, mounted, and started north toward Monterey at a hard run.

The sound of his fading hooves stirred panic in Maria Inés. Men would soon arrive and the Americanos would not believe her if she claimed the gold was hers, hidden many years ago. They would say she had helped in the murdering of Señora Reed and they would hang her like they had done the Indian who merely carried a letter for Señor Piloto Reed. They would not understand this was blood money of a kind. Payment from Esperanza and her husband for the purchase of her son. She saw it clearly now.

Scratching with the stone until her fingers bled, she began digging a hole, softening the earth with her tears. With numbed fingers she chipped at the dry soil, digging deeper and deeper until it was large enough to hold the stiff leather thong of her buried gold. When she was satisfied that the gold was again hidden safely, she pushed the earth back and packed it firmly, using a piece of bark to scrape the mound smooth of finger marks. Then, with her burden basket in a loose strap over her shoulder, she rose and began half-walking, half-running, in a zigzag path through the sagebrush.

She ran through the afternoon, listening for the sound of thundering hooves behind her. The road she traveled was chewed with the dust of a thousand travelers, one of which had killed her husband. Somewhere beneath the layers of dust were the small footprints of her son when he had left years before. Now he was a grown man. She would not know him if he were to ride past her on the road.

CHAPTER EIGHTEEN

The night was alive with the sounds of crickets and rustling birds, even though the road was empty of travelers. Each dark shape seemed to be a murderer lying in wait for her. She tasted fear in her mouth, but she continued walking because she was too afraid to stop.

The moon was rising in the east when she came upon a small caravan of immigrants from Sonora who had arrived in Alta California just as hungry American gold miners spread out across the Sacramento basin and demanded a steep tax of the Mexicans for the privilege of searching for their gold— sometimes even the forfeit of their lives. Now they had turned back, looking for land in the south where it was safer. She approached the woman and offered to trade her labor for the right to camp beside them—and after conferring with her husband, the woman agreed.

The caravan camped at the rancho adobe where the Mission sheepherders lived while they tended the flocks. Afterwards, a Mexican family settled there, but the family had been unable to provide proof of their ownership and the Yanqui government forced them off of the land. The new owners were Americans and they did not understand the hospitality required of them. They allowed the horses to be watered and the oxen to graze on the dried summer grass, but they did not offer to butcher one of their cattle to feed the hungry travelers. Instead, Maria Inés helped to lay out a cold meal of dried fruits and jerked beef and tortillas, with only cold water to drink instead of coffee, but she had not eaten in two days and the food tasted like a feast.

The talk around the campfire was agitated. A dozen of Señor Rios's riders had spread out across the countryside, warning settlers of the murders, and everyone had news of the massacred souls at San Miguel, each claiming to have the true story.

"I spoke to a man who came upon the murders and only escaped because at the last moment the missing bell in the tower rang out in a miraculous manner and the murderers fled for their lives."

"Fifteen Indians were seen fleeing the Mission with gold chains around their necks. Greasy Indians."

Maria Inés shuddered and gave thanks that she had returned her gold to the earth.

"There were women in the rooms who entertained men. Surely they invited the violence. Why else would there be so many women and only two men?"

One thing puzzled her, but she attributed it to gossip, as well.

"They say one small boy is unaccounted for. The grandson of Olivera, the Indian. He was not found among the dead. They say he ran off into the sage. They are searching for him in the fields."

"Maybe the men had a change of heart and allowed the child to live."

Maria Inés drew her shawl over her shoulders against the sudden chill sweeping her body.

The sun was a long way from chasing away the cold night when they rose and prepared for their journey. The owners of the rancho watched them depart as though they were going to steal the gates off the fences—or the gold off their fingers. Maria Inés shook the dust from her sandals and spat in the dirt as she departed.

The roadside through the Rancho El Paso de Robles was

dark with mustard stems as far as the eye could see. The hungry animals tore at them whenever they could reach a patch, but the nourishing yellow mustard flowers were absent. As she walked she remembered eating the mustard out of hunger, like the animals, but she said nothing to the woman and her children. They would find out soon enough what the future held for them.

At the place where she had camped once with her husband on their way to the Asistencia at Santa Margarita, she closed her eyes and searched her pack for her rosary. For many miles she walked beside the carreta, fingering her beads and praying so the nightmare of the murders did not revive itself in her mind.

The oxen moved so slowly that she had to slow her steps so she did not outdistance the cart. As she walked she had time to study the land. The new grass was already pushing through the ground to cover the hills with the color of life. Across the valley a few scattered animals were feeding on hillsides terraced by hooves of thousands of cattle now gone. The Mexican señor and his son rode back and forth, searching the arroyos for water and canyons for places where bandidos might hide out—and with good reason. The men they met on the road had a desperate, hungry look to them. Many were Yanquis fresh from the gold mines, the same sort as had stopped at the Mission. Each time one of them looked in her direction she shrank from sight and covered her face with her shawl so her fear did not show. Thanks be to God, the men did not approach the laden carts, probably out of regard for the small children who hung over the edges and stared at them with curious eyes.

In late morning a mounted band of riders galloped past, bound for the Mission by the look of them—and heedless of the adobe mud churned up by their horses. One carried a spade tied behind his cantle, for burying the bodies, it appeared. Either that or they were going to search for the gold.

At the marshy place the Mexicans had named Atascadero, Maria Inés slowed her steps so that the caravan continued on without her. Without telling anyone, she turned into the setting sun, onto an ancient trail her ancestors used to travel. She had never been to the sacred place of the People's beginning. Her mother had told her of the place. Now she would visit the birthplace of her ancestors.

The trail was easy through the oaks, the ground covered with so many acorns, even the squirrels had enough. She spent precious time filling her basket and cracking them with a stone, pounding the meat into meal on a flat rock and pressing the pulp into her basket. She took a taste, but the bitterness brought a pucker to her mouth. She would wait to reach the creek.

For a day's walk the trail was straight and level, the trees far enough apart that she could see a grizzly before it was upon her. Small creatures crashed through the underbrush, their footfalls in the dried leaves sounding like a much larger animal. Again and again she looked behind her, fearful of a predator, but each time the trail was empty. Even so, the strain of caution made the day seem long. Never had she been so far from the Mission. Even on short journeys the escolte had been along with their pistolas and long guns.

She smiled as she spoke her thought aloud. "How Grandmother would laugh. She would call me one of the *light-eyes.*" Her smile quickly faded. "What good are the padres' ways if they cannot help me now?"

She kept to the trail along the creek, past a rushing waterfall where she leached her acorn mash. Afterwards she ate a handful, savoring the buttery taste. Grandmother had described this sacred place with awe in her voice as she told stories of how the old ones had bound their dead on a log, and with great ceremony, set it into the water at the top of the falls and allowed the body to return to the sea.

Above the rushing waterfall, Grandmother nodded approvingly. She indicated a stick good for digging roots and waited until Maria Inés picked it up and put it into her burden basket before she disappeared.

After a rest, Maria Inés continued on the ancient trail as it wound over a knob-shaped rise and began descending into a valley with a small lake. While the evening stole sunlight from the day she searched for dry branches she could weave into a tight hut. Afterwards she prepared her bed of fragrant evergreen boughs. She drank from the cold water, but she didn't eat any of the dried jerky or acorns because her supply was nearly gone.

Near the small creek she found the remains of summer's gooseberries, their fruit shriveled to hard, seedy balls. Their tartness caused her mouth to salivate, but they filled her belly. At first she chewed the pulp and spit out the seeds, but she was so hungry that she eventually swallowed the hard nuggets without tasting them.

The valley held camas roots, wild onions, and elderberries. Other plants grew under the oaks and she picked those she recognized, and filled her basket with pine nuts. Some distance from her camp she picked a handful of wild rose hips and held them to her nose. The smell reminded her of Grandmother.

The next morning she set off along a ridge overgrown with chamise and sage that had not seen fire in many years. Thorns plucked at her clothing and skin. The cold bit at her, but she continued walking because she did not want to be caught on the ridge trail when night fell. At every bend in the canyon trail she feared meeting a grizzly, but God was with her and she saw only a tawny mountain lion watching her from an outcropping. She saw the curiosity in its eyes.

"Hello, little brother," she called. "We walk together. You will not hurt me because we are one."

Maria Inés

Still, she was glad when it turned and bounded away.

As she walked she recalled a story her mother had told her about the world in the time of Padre Serra. The padre's new community at the small Mission San Carlos was struggling, his neophytes starving, and it was not yet the growing season. The pagan Indians there were unfriendly and did not help to find food. Even the soldados were starving. Padre Serra was afraid for his people, but then he remembered a valley they had passed through on their journey north, a place they had named Los Osos for its many grizzlies. He sent his escolte down to this place and they killed so many bears with their long guns that they filled several carretas with the meat and brought it back to San Carlos. He explained to the neophytes that the bear was not their brother—it was not a taboo like they had been told by their ancestors; the white God would allow them to eat the meat they believed to be sacred. They believed him and they did not starve.

From the top of the mountain, she could see the clear blue waters of the bay. The air was salty and pleasant, unlike the monjério where the air had been dead. At the horizon a fog bank extended for as far as she could see, like a monster waiting to pounce. Far down the beach stood *Le Sa Mo,* the huge rock where the ancestors claimed her people began—when they swam as fish from the sea and learned to walk onto the land.

She recalled a prayer of her people. "We see you in the *morro,* in the ocean, in the sun, in the moon. We hear you in the kingfisher, in the coyote, in our songs. Thank you, *Hianisponica.*"

The morro filled the bay like a whale surrounded by gentle lapping waves ending in a crescent of white sand. Her father had told her stories of the ocean and the sand, and the creatures living there. He had said that many were good for eating, but his stories did not tell of a world where sea birds skimmed the surface of the water, plucking small fish from a vast ocean that

189

carried the padres from a distant land. Beyond the waves, otters floated on their backs, prying shells open and then tipping the contents into their mouths. In the distance, a group of whales swam south, now and again sending up plumes of water from their backs.

She stood watching as the afternoon sun made its slow journey into the sea and the mountain became painted with the hues of dusk. This day had begun with only the thought to be off the trail by sunset, but now she saw the world below her and she felt one with the creatures she watched. As the sun touched the water's edge she continued down the trail, off the hillside of golden grass and onto the soft sand sifting beneath her toes. She cupped her hand and took a drink of the frothy water, and spit it out when she tasted the salt.

The wind had picked up in the late afternoon and now it blew the warmth of the sun away. Her belly was growling from hunger. She saw a creature crawling along the sand and she picked it up and dashed its hard shell against a stone and pulled the insides out with her fingers. The meat was nutty and delicious, so she hunted for another.

The nearby tide pools teemed with life, and she moved from one to another, prying shells from the rocks and cracking them open. Some she spit out and did not try again, but others tasted good.

From the corner of her eye she saw a shadowy figure lumber out from the trees. An immense grizzly leading a cub waded into the water and stood to its haunches in a bowl-shaped tide pool swirling with fish and crabs trapped by the low tide. The mother bear crouched and began eating. Fortunately, Maria Inés was upwind and the bear was turned toward the waves, but when it rose to its full height and let out a bellow, the sound shook the earth. She remained frozen, praying to God for safety while the grizzly ambled away on all fours, shaking its head back and forth as it led its cub back over the rocky ridges. A sea otter sunning itself gave a bark of surprise and the grizzly changed its course. With a single swipe of its huge claw, the bear made its kill.

Maria Inés stole quietly toward a small mountain of plant-covered sand where she could hide until the bear and its cub ambled away. That night her bed was a hollow made in the side of the dune, out of the wind, where the sand was still warm from the sun.

The next day she followed the track until she came to a place where the sea had nibbled away the trail and she could travel no farther. She looked at the hills that grew from the water's edge, but she was too weary to climb. Instead, she found a place on the beach where the charging surf woke her and lulled her back to sleep again, over and over with the gentle sounds of a mother's hushing.

Cayucos was the name the Mexicans had given this place.

In the morning the sea had spit out the land again. She continued forward on sand that was hard and wet, crowded with small sea creatures for her morning meal.

She found a fish struggling on the sand and she ate it without building a cooking fire. Later she nibbled the kelp. It was salty and she spread it out to dry. She picked up a knob of bull kelp shaped like the shaker instruments the boys used when they made music at the Mission. She plucked a few from the kelp and put them in her basket for drying.

The tide began to rise again and she walked quickly north until the trail climbed upward in a slow, steady rise. When she reached the higher ground she paused to rest where she could watch the otters playing in the waves, and beyond, a line of great black whales making their way south. The day was clear and eternal, like God was just above, smiling on this paradise. She thought of her son living all these years in the shadow of this beauty with Esperanza and Jose Toma, and she felt the burn of jealousy in her breast.

During the night a heavy rain fed the land. It followed her all the next day, drenching her clothing, but she did not slow her pace, even when torrents clawed at the trail, eroding the depressions of her footprints cushioned in the sand. Beginning in the early hours, the smells of the fresh earth mingled with those from the sea and filled the air with the fullness of life. By morning the rain had swabbed out all history of sandals, boots, and bare feet in the hard-packed sand.

At a point where the trail curved between two hills she took shelter in an overhang where the brush was dry enough to kindle. At first the chunk of flint was clumsy in her stiff fingers, but she lit a small flame and added bits of driftwood until the fire warmed her bones. Deadwood from nearby oaks fed the fire for many hours until her clothes were dry and the chill left her body. She slept well that night.

The rain was gone when she started out the next morning. Unlike the adobe clay of the Mission, this sandy soil was thirsty for the rain. A rainbow had formed and the sun glistened on the blue water with such intensity that she had to squint to see.

By afternoon the trail turned inward toward the mountains. This trail was more recent. She felt her steps grow lighter because she knew she was near the end of her journey. She saw a cow on the hillside, grazing the terraced trail. Soon the hills were dotted with dozens of cattle, sheep, and horses. She continued walking until she heard the sound of chopping wood and a man's voice, calling.

Rafael Villa's rancho bustled with activity. She stood at the edge of the trail and watched as an Indian woman hung laundry on bushes. Despite the lateness of the season, a garden still produced squash, corn, peppers, and onions. In the nearby orchard, orange and lemon trees were laden with fruit, but it was their scent that drove her quickly in their direction. Without hesitation she made her way to the nearest tree, pulled two oranges down, and began peeling one with shaking fingers. As soon as she finished she began on the second, slowing to savor the juices on her tongue.

A pile of clamshells lay heaped near a log where someone had been cleaning them. Smoke rose from a half-dozen cook stoves and she imagined she could smell stew cooking in someone's pot. Tears clouded her vision at the sight of a young vaquero breaking a horse, his brown skin gleaming with sweat. She clasped her arms around her middle and waited for a glimpse of the boy's face, hoping for a hint of his father's proud cheekbones. When the boy pulled the horse to a halt and slipped off, she walked the remaining steps and stood at the edge of the corral, searching his eyes hoping to see something familiar, but there was nothing. Backing away, she turned toward the row of huts and waited for someone to greet her.

CHAPTER NINETEEN

A small man approached, his shy smile filling his brown face with kindness. His clothes were torn and poor, but they were clean and had been neatly, if inexpertly, patched. He doffed his hat when he reached her, a gesture both humbling and inexplicably proud.

"*Shaamo'sh,* my sister. Welcome. You have walked far. Come, eat before you make a bed of the trail you stand on."

She smiled and the burden of the journey she had taken did not seem so great. "It was not far," she said.

He nodded, his eyes serious. "I know you from the time of Padre Cabot."

She dipped her head. Too many memories fought inside her. He did not seem to care that she was without words, but continued to lead her to a makeshift hut where a pan simmered on the fire.

"Venison stew. It will bring your voice back again," he said.

His voice held the hint of humor and she looked up, surprised. She said nothing as she ate the thick chunks of meat and corn that he handed her in an abalone shell, better than any she could remember.

"No pozole. You are disappointed?"

She shook her head and a smile fitted the corners of her mouth.

He turned away to fetch more wood so she could eat in peace. When he returned he added to the fire and straightened without looking at her directly. She saw a bow and a quiver of arrows hanging from a thong.

"Did you kill the deer with those?" She heard the rusty, unused tone in her voice and remembered it had been many days since she had spoken.

"It is not a big deer, but thanks be to God, it will feed us well."

She looked up, for the first time directly at him, and saw the happiness lighting his face. It was a moment like when she had first heard Padre Cabot speak inside the church.

"Thanks be to God." Her throat was scratchy with the effort. He didn't seem to notice and she turned to see where she might go for shelter. He seemed to know her need and he nodded in the direction of a small adobe.

She rose and left her empty dish and nearly stumbled in her exhaustion, past a woman bent over in the garden. The woman rose and raised a hand to her eyes, shading herself from the setting sun.

"Maria Inés?"

Maria Inés saw the surprised expression on Esperanza's face, even though the hand hid her features. Her hair had grown long, braided and wrapped around her temples. She was wearing a wool tunic like they had woven at the Mission. Maria Inés nodded and looked around to see if her friend had other children playing nearby, but there were only the small boys at the corral watching the vaqueros working the horses. It was hard to know with boys this age because each wanted to be independent of their mothers.

Esperanza took hold of the vegetables she had harvested and started toward the adobe. "Come. We will talk while I prepare the meal. Jose Toma will be here soon."

Jose Toma? No mention of Miguelito? She followed without speaking until they reached the room. The door was low. A tall man like Miguelito, surely, would have to bend if he were to enter.

Inside, she joined Esperanza at a low table and they began scrubbing squash for baking beneath the coals. The minutes passed and still she could think of nothing to say. It was for Esperanza to say her son's name, not hers.

"He is not here." The words sliced the air like a knife, but Maria Inés gave no indication she heard. She continued rubbing the squash until it was smooth, then set it aside and picked up another.

"You came to see him, but he's not here. Many months ago he left to work at Rancho El Paso de Robles. I think he is there, but I have not heard."

Maria Inés looked up and she stilled her hands. "I have come far. Now I must go back."

Esperanza frowned. "Stay with us for a while. It is good here. We have plenty to eat and we practice the old ways, those we remember. The men have a sweathouse. We make adobe houses and the men dance at night and make music the old way. It is not like the old days, but it is good because we are together."

Maria Inés considered. "I will remain here until it is time to leave."

Esperanza smiled. "Put your things over here. We are happy to share our quarters with you."

The man she had met when she first arrived was named Ygnacio. He brought her a gift of a fat possum and left it at the door for her to find. She smiled as she cleaned it and cut it up for the pot. The gift made her feel like she was not a burden and she was grateful.

The following day she joined the women who were carding wool to be spun into thread for a blanket.

"I saw sheep on my journey," she told them.

Esperanza continued feeding the carded wool into her spindle. "The air is different here. The wool is softer because the sun is not so intense. It is good to have the sheep because we have no flax. We use dogbane for our cordage, the same as in the olden times."

"You trade with the trading ships?"

Esperanza shrugged. "We earn money where we can. It is different for the young men. They are paid silver for their skills. Our young men are the finest horsemen in all of California."

Maria Inés remembered the work she did for Señora Rios and the small things she received in exchange. But never silver or coin. "Maybe I will live in this place."

Esperanza smiled. "It is good to have news of the world. Tell us about the Mission and everything you know."

Maria Inés began hesitantly. Storytelling seemed strange at first, for she was not a person of words.

In the evenings around the campfire, Ygnacio leaned closer to hear her slow, halting story of the murders at the Mission and she found herself adding details to bring the story alive. Each night she had something to share that the people hadn't heard, about the governor or the Americans—news that would change their futures. She told of how the Americans dishonored Mexican land grants because the owners did not have a paper to prove their ownership. The men and the women listened intently, and they accepted her. In her soft, warm wool tunic she felt safer than in many years.

On the day of the winter solstice, a week after she arrived, they loaded corn and chilies onto an old horse and Ygnacio led it to the morro of their beginning while Maria Inés carried a blackberry pie. They climbed the rock and lit a fire and prayed. Sang the old songs and remembered how it was to be a People. When they grew hungry they dug for clams. The boys dove into the chilly water to pry abalone off the rocks while the women dug a pit in the sand and made a fire of driftwood. When it was burned to coals, they added the seafood and the corn and chilies, all wrapped in kelp. The men covered the fire and let it cook. When it was ready they brought out the food and spread it onto an old hide, careful not to burn themselves with the steam.

Later, men began to play their music while, one by one, others rose and began shuffling their feet in the sand to the rhythm of the simple instruments. Maria Inés joined them. Singing the old songs, watching the traditional dances accompanied by whistles and drums formed by their own hands, made her remember being at her mother's side, watching as her father danced and played at the fiestas. She brought out one of the bull kelp rattles she had painted and decorated with bits of shells tied to a string of doeskin, and the boys used it for the dance.

Later, Ygnacio caught up with her as she walked along the water.

"The pie has been eaten."

"It is good to have enough. No one will be hungry." She smiled to herself because he was too polite to say it was delicious. "Maybe you were too full to have any?" she teased.

He acted embarrassed. "I did not throw my share to the dogs."

She felt like a girl again, making him blush. "This is good. The dogs get fat and they will not watch for possums in the garden."

Ygnacio walked beside her for a long way before he spoke again. "There is a padre again at San Antonio."

She had heard this. "A Mexican," she said.

"But still, a priest. Padre Ambris. They say he is a reasonable man."

She acted as though she didn't understand his reasoning. "There will be baptisms now."

"Maybe marriages—if anyone has the need."

"Who would be foolish enough to marry in these times?"

"That is for the woman to say." Ygnacio was not to be deterred. He did not look up, but he did not turn back, either.

She liked the way he matched his footsteps to hers as they walked farther down the beach, neither talking. Finally it was time to turn back. "In the monjério, if the priest were to ask who she wanted to marry, sometimes a girl would say 'the one who stands outside my window.' "

"That is a good way."

"I will marry you because you are a good man and I am tired of sleeping on a cold mat."

Chapter Twenty

The carreta crept along the ridge trail, the wheels sliding over remnants of mud on the slippery slope. The land to the west of the ridges, from the mountains to the sea, was interlaid with smaller ridges that looked, from a distance, as though they had been created by the folds of whiskey-colored cloth. Here and there a scrub oak struggled in the unaccommodating soil of the west slope, barren of trees. Madrone and oak grew in the fleshy folds of the ridges, giving the land the impression of verdant life. On the ridges, clumps of manzanita, chamise, and pea chaparral hid a buck and a doe in the low whiskey grass. A pair of hawks flew east toward their nesting tree. Maria Inés filled her basket with miner's lettuce growing under the oaks. Soon they were over the top of the first hill and the land opened to deep forests and pockets of loamy soil.

Maria Inés and the other Indians walked, carrying their possessions in ragged burden baskets. They followed the few Mexicans on horses who rode ahead of carretas filled with bedding and provisions for the eight days of the Easter fiesta. The caravan halted often so the drivers could grease the overheated axles of sycamore wood with his supply of tallow.

Ygnacio walked beside her, his eyes concerned when he saw the way she craned ahead for a view of the Mission San Antonio.

"The grounds will not look like it did," he warned. "Many of the tiles were sold."

Maria Inés nodded, pressing her lips together to hide her sorrow. "Maybe it would have been better if a white family had taken it for their residence like at San Miguel." *But maybe not.* She closed her eyes at the memory of the Reed family.

He walked silently without meeting her eye. "You will be saddened by what you see. The adobe walls are sliding back into the earth."

"But there will be new life as well. Wait and see."

When the caravan reached San Antonio, Maria Inés halted to stare. Only the gardens and orchards, and the church itself, remained. No blacksmith shop or tavern profaned its walls like travelers reported of San Miguel. Instead, thirty-five Salinan families were living in the neophyte rooms and the small buildings they had built from old adobe walls. New fields held vegetable plants to feed them through the summer. Orchards and vineyards were alive with pink and white blossoms. A donkey was turning the grist mill, grinding corn. Children sang and laughed as they ran through the courtyard tossing sticks through a hoop.

The surrounding grounds already held many carts and campfires of people who had arrived from the surrounding ranchos. Mexicans, Indians, and some Americano families had hung blankets over ropes to give their women privacy.

She felt her eyes stinging as she heard the lilt of a priest calling out to his visitors. His voice was old and feeble, and he walked with a painful limp as if it hurt to take even a single step, but his spirit was strong.

The crisp tang of new earth filled her nostrils. For a moment she closed her eyes and her heart heard the slow cadence of the brick makers patting adobe into wooden forms. She heard the clink of hoe against rock from the workers in the garden, the laughter and singing of the women as they worked spinning wool into habit cloth for the padre—every sound created in her the false sense that life was as it had been. For a moment she could believe Lacero would soon be coming in from his work to swing his son into the air and chuck him under the chin as he sang his song and danced the steps of the owl dance for the boy to learn the words; *"pa'-na-ta pa'-na-ta co'ko-na!"* Dance, owl, dance.

She smiled as the weariness of the journey fell away. With a start she realized Ygnacio was watching, his eyes sad for her.

Afterwards, when her husband-to-be left her side to attend to the livestock, the priest limped toward her with a smile. "Welcome, my daughter. I am Padre Ambris."

She saw his worn black habit and wondered why he did not cover his head with a cowl the way the padres had done. In a few months when the dry summer heat burned his nostrils, he would need a hat. She did not look up to meet his eyes, for he was of Mexican descent and she was shy around strangers.

The priest seemed to sense this. "Come, you must be hungry. By the grace of God, many of the new arrivals have something to offer you. We will eat together."

Ygnacio arrived back at her side and stood respectfully, holding his worn reed sombrero in his hands. He waited until the padre turned to him before he said in a quiet, proud tone, "We wish to be married, Padre. This woman and myself."

The padre nodded, pleased. "On the Easter feast we will hold a wedding celebration for everyone who desires."

The first morning she walked around and saw the familiar oaks, some bearing new leaves, others dusty and tired from wearing their old coat through the winter. Some of the trees would bear acorns, but others merely shaded the ground for travelers. The air was clean and dry, the mornings clear of fog, unlike the rancho near the sea. She breathed deeply and felt a wave of homesickness rolling through her.

Ygnacio looked up from where he was playing a gambling game with some of the other men, punctuated with much laughter and teasing. He did not rise to join her, and she was glad he remained. He was with the men and she was free to share news with the other women.

Señor Rios and his family had arrived and an Indian woman was preparing their evening meal. His children were playing with the children of other Mexican families and the children of their servants, each of them involved in a game of kick-the-ball—all of them barefoot. Maria Inés did not present herself to the Señora, but she did not shy away, either. Her work there was from another time. Today was today.

Maria Inés recognized girls she had grown up with at San Miguel and her heart lifted at the memory of sharing the women's quarters with them. One of her favorites, Perfecta Encinales, had arrived with her brood of children. She stood for a few minutes watching as her friend directed her children in the unpacking of their supplies. God had blessed Perfecta with a home and many children, and for a moment Maria Inés felt the flutter of envy deep inside her gut. Even though their home was only a half-day's travel, the family camped with the others so their older children could spend time with others of their age. Her husband Eucebio was also in attendance, the couple like royalty because everyone knew them.

The women had a hog roasting over coals in a pit dug in the ground. Once it was uncovered and the women started slicing, the aromas filled the air.

Perfecta looked over, recognized her, and smiled. "Come. Eat. It is good to see a face from the old days, Maria Inés. You are well?"

Maria Inés reached for a piece of pork with her fingers and let the scent fill her senses. She returned the smile and her envy dissipated. "Padre Cabot used to eat pork cooked this way," she said, knowing her words would be accepted as a compliment.

Perfecta's face reflected the strain of remembering back so

many years. "There was much to eat in those days." She looked about her and beckoned to a pair of hungry looking Indians crouching at the edge of the campfire. "Come. There is enough for everyone."

The two hurried over without taking their eyes from the ground. She sliced off two generous hunks which they eagerly accepted. One had lost his teeth and he pulled the meat into thin strips with his fingers. He chewed deliberately, his eyes already searching for more. Their hands were filthy, their clothing reduced to ragged loincloths over scant sinew and bone. Maria Inés tried to place them, but the two scarecrows in front of her were from another time. "Where do you stay?" she asked gently. One of them motioned toward the brushy hillside. In the morning she would see if any of the others had a blanket or a pair of trousers to spare.

Perfecta had the same idea. She returned to her cart and pulled a used hat like the ones she wove from reeds, this one showing hard use. She put it on the tongue of the carreta and returned to her food. One of the men advanced and picked it up. Twisting it in his hands, he shuffled off into the dark.

Sprinkled throughout the camp, in the light of a dozen lanterns, Indians gambled with dice and shells, their laughter comforting and familiar. Maria Inés smiled when she saw Ygnacio's profile against a blanket hanging in one of the camps. She walked slowly past the carretas, looking for familiar faces. Some of the women she had thought dead were there with husbands and families, but too many were missing for her to feel with a full heart. One thought kept echoing inside her head. *We are so few.*

On her second pass through the camp she no longer pretended she was not searching for her son. She wrapped her shawl around her in the brisk night air and wandered from one group of young men to another, looking for a handsome boy with high cheekbones and a vaquero's quick laugh.

"He will be here tomorrow." Esperanza had walked up behind her.

Maria Inés said nothing. She did not want to give Esperanza the satisfaction of thinking she was right. A race was planned for the next day. Her son would surely want to show off his skills.

She was up before the others, before the sun crossed the top of the hill, washing herself in the canal that ran through the Mission lands from the San Miguel Creek. To have water without having to carry it was a blessing. Nevertheless, she carried a basketful back to the camp. They would need it for cooking the acorn mush with the rocks heating in the embers. So many skills she had learned from the others living at the Villa Rancho. Some knew a little of this, others remembered a different lesson. They shared their knowledge and many of the old ways were returning.

She had not told Ygnacio, but she was not planning to return to the ranch. Each time she looked at Esperanza she saw only betrayal. Padre Cabot would not want her to live with such venomous thoughts. After they married she would tell Ygnacio about her plan to return to San Miguel.

The rodeo would take place in a few hours. Not as big as the one held in September to celebrate Mexico's independence, but still, exciting. This day, the races would be between the Mexican and Indian vaqueros. They would have fancy riding feats in front of everyone to see who had the greatest nerve. Already the small roosters were being readied for burying in the sand so the men could pluck them out by their heads at a run. She smiled, remembering when Lacero had won the prize.

She returned to the camp to see to the fruit pies she had baked for this day. Someone was baking bread in the adobe horno near the cookhouse. She inhaled the scent of Padre

Cabot's favorite treat, good wheat bread served with homemade butter and honey from the apiary. For a moment, with her eyes closed, it seemed as though nothing had changed.

Ygnacio stood beside her at the races. He had bet his lariat on one of the horses and he could not afford to lose it, but the offer had been made and he would not refuse. None of the men would. It was their women who would suffer at the end of the day, but the men would have their honor.

A sorrel stallion pranced in eagerness at the starting line, ridden by a vaquero with the grace and fluidity of a high-born Spanish Don. But the man was not wealthy. His clothing was poor and his boots were worn from use. Maria Inés looked at his shaded features under his flat-brimmed hat and her heart took a quick beat. *It was him!* She would recognize the easy smile anywhere, the daring machismo of his father.

"Which horse do you bet on?" she asked Ygnacio, to have something to occupy her.

"This one. Miguelito. I have known him since he was a child." She winced at the easy way he spoke as he nodded in the horse's direction. "Jose Toma's son." He could not know how the words sliced through her heart. For a moment she considered remaining silent, but Padre Cabot words filled her with resolve.

"He is *my* son."

Ygnacio turned to look at her and her face convulsed with many emotions. His own softened with understanding and he patted her tenderly.

"From this day forward, your pain will be my pain."

She felt his body resting so near to hers, his arm warm on her shoulder and she felt herself relax. It had been so long since she had felt a man's touch. Now her prayers had come to be. She remained silent, but her smile spoke for her.

The horse won easily. Her son rode over the finish line with his sombrero held high above his head as though the effort of winning took nothing from him. Ygnacio soon returned with his lariat slung over his shoulder and a smaller one clasped in his hand.

Maria Inés followed the rider with her eyes, waiting for a chance to speak to him, but he was busy winning other races and receiving the accolades of his friends. She was surprised to see him in the company of several Mexican vaqueros, many garbed in short leather jackets decorated with silver conchos. Even their boots were decorated with silver. Her son had none, but his style made him more handsome than the men with their riches.

She waited until he approached the area where the food was spread out. Every man worried first about his stomach and her son was no different.

"Miguelito?"

The boy looked up and his eyes discarded her worn clothing and her hopeful eyes.

"Miguelito?" She said his name a second time, glad for the chance to hear it rolling off her tongue. "My son, I have waited many years for this moment." This time he did not look at her, only stiffened and waited for her to continue. "I am your mother. Do you not remember?"

He turned and his eyes blazed with anger. "You are not my mother," he spat. "You are a squaw! My father was a high-born Mexican caballero who was dispossessed of his land. Jose Toma has told me the truth. I am Mexican."

She waited for him to see his mistake and to lower his head for a blessing, but he did neither. Instead he turned to his friends, laughing as he walked in the direction of the beef roasting over the coals. He said something and the other boy glanced back at where she stood blinking back tears.

She did not remember eating. She sat with the others in a circle of people crouched on the dirt. She must have taken food when it was passed, but she did not remember touching any of it. Someone poured liquid into her gourd, but the taste of it soured in her stomach. Several times she saw the boy, Miguelito, but he looked away before she could implore him with her eyes to come to her. Praise God, the day passed with the ordinary chores of serving and cleaning up until it was time for sleeping.

The wedding was held following the Easter Mass, after the orchestra played the sacred hymns and the old padre gave a joyous sermon about becoming reborn. She attended confession on Holy Saturday to prepare herself, and she forgave her son for his rejection.

At the *fandango,* the informal dance that followed, she danced *jotas* and *zambras* with the other women, and quadrilles until her feet were sore and her throat tired from laughing in an effort to forget her anger on her wedding day. It was hard to forgive Esperanza, for she saw her son eating with the woman and her husband, Jose Toma.

Ygnacio found them a place near the garden where they could be alone for the night. When morning came she returned to her camp to make preparations. Esperanza was there, folding the bedding and placing it in the carreta for the return trip over the mountain. Maria Inés said nothing as she gathered her possessions and packed them inside the burden basket she had carried from San Miguel.

Esperanza, too, worked without speaking. Others hurried to put the camp to rights, for the trip was long and they wanted to be on the trail soon after daybreak. When she finished packing, Ygnacio waited for her to begin their journey. She followed him out of hearing before she spoke. "I do not return to the rancho. There is something I must do. You may go with me or you may not, it does not matter. I must do this thing."

Her husband studied her with such intensity that she felt like a ripe melon split open by the sun. She was surprised to feel her heart pounding as she waited for his answer. When he slowly nodded, she quietly released the breath she had been holding.

Chapter Twenty-One

The trail south to San Miguel was peppered with travelers returning home from Mission San Antonio and others traveling north—Americans in Conestoga wagons and simple Mexican families in their ancient carretas filled with children. She and Ygnacio walked for a week, pausing to rest often in the spring grass and mustard. The trails were barely dry, the adobe rutted from the passing wagons, but the air was fresh and alive. She was grateful her husband asked no questions because she found it hard to talk about the rock in her heart. He had seen the way Esperanza laughed with her son. He understood.

She passed the place where Lacero had been murdered. Because the sun was setting when they reached the river, she led the way and watched as Ygnacio knelt and said a prayer over the sandy mound. It was good, having both of her men together in this way. It was as though a circle had been made and she was part of it.

Ygnacio asked her if she would like him to gather the bones and take them to San Miguel where he could bury them. She considered for several minutes. The Mission did not seem to be a holy place anymore. The padres were gone and there was the rowdiness of the tavern and the desecration to consider. She shook her head.

"He is happy here. This is land he knows."

Ygnacio nodded and did not challenge her decision, even though she knew it would not be the choice he made for himself.

210

When it was his time she would bury him at the Mission.

They arrived at San Miguel late in the afternoon and she felt a shiver of fear run through her. The portico was damaged, the thatched roof bare in places where the wind had torn the covering off. Some of the outbuildings had tiles removed and the adobe bricks were melting back into the earth where they had come from. She saw everything from a distance because she could not bear to walk where the murderers had walked. The doors on the outside were closed, but in her mind she saw them as they had been that night, open with lantern light spilling out.

People were living and working in the rooms now, but even activity and life could not erase the images from her mind. She allowed Ygnacio to lead the way into a copse of sycamores by the river where the willows hid them from strangers.

When a thin sliver of moon rose over the hill and started its dance toward morning, she woke and drew her shawl around her shoulders. Ygnacio rose as well and they started creeping forward, as silently as two deer.

In the darkness the trees were dense and dark, and she was glad because she did not have to wonder about shadows she could not see. Her eyes were good in the darkness, better than even Lacero's had been. She knew where she was going because she had gone there many times in her dreams.

At the oak tree she knelt and began digging with the stick she used for finding roots. Many years had packed the soil, but the latest spring rains had not yet dried the earth. She hit a rock and for a moment her heart caught, but she continued digging, slowly and carefully in case the leather sack had rotted from moisture. When the stick would go no farther she knew the leather had stiffened in the dry soil until it was as hard as a rock. She dug the hole wider and reached in to grasp the sack. It came out with difficulty, the stiff edges catching on the dirt. She wrapped it in her shawl and pushed dirt back into the hole, then brushed leaves across the top to erase any sign.

The journey back to the river was made with caution. Ygnacio led the way, stopping often to be sure no one followed. She did not open the sack because she needed the light of a fire to see. Time enough at first light.

The next morning she bored a hole through the leather. Ygnacio watched silently as she poured the contents into a leather sack she had sewed for just this purpose. Together they watched the gold dust spill out. After a moment he asked, "What will you do with it?"

"It belongs to my son. I will take it to him." She watched Ygnacio's eyes to see what sort of man she had married and she was happy when his mouth relaxed and he nodded.

On the ride south to the Rancho El Paso de Robles, she told him the story of how she had acquired the money. He chuckled when he heard how Esperanza had stolen from the thieves.

"I know now they were buying my son. I should not have taken it."

He frowned and his eyes turned thoughtful. "Do not have such thoughts about your friend. Maybe it was God's will for him. At the ranch he grew up knowing many things that will help him survive."

"He is my son, not hers."

"He calls himself a Mexican because the law protects these people. There is no punishment for killing an Indian. But his heart knows the truth. No matter who rules the land, we are still slaves."

She did not answer because there was nothing to say. Her husband was right in this. But her son would have gold to change his destiny. She would do this for him.

At the head of a canyon, where a ranchería had stood in the days before the Missions, many Indians had built huts and were growing small plots of vegetables, but the land was poor and the soil they had been given did not support the many people who lived there. A pair of deer antlers hung from a tree. Some of the people looked as though they had been living there for many months, ragged and half-starving. Maria Inés recognized some of them, but others had changed so much they seemed strangers. Young men and women had grown into old men and women who no longer smiled. Some sat weaving reeds into baskets, but their eyes were clouded with fatigue.

One man had died the night before and his friends were preparing a grave with sticks and branches.

Maria Inés carried her digging stick to a place near the river where other women were searching for roots. After the funeral ceremony Ygnacio returned with a nest of small mice for the stew she was preparing. A woman with a small child approached, holding out a handful of mustard greens and Maria Inés added them to the pot with some more water. Soon another woman offered a large camas root and a handful of wild onions. There were more mouths than food. Those who ate did so with their eyes down, trying to ignore the hungry eyes of others watching. It was all Maria Inés could do to swallow the food, for she was not used to the meat, but others were hungry and so she ate.

Ygnacio found an ancient mare who was too tired to keep up with the herd of wild horses that had come to the river to drink. He spent many hours creeping up on it and managed to wrap a worn rope around its neck. The mare did not struggle. Perhaps it felt its time was near.

Ygnacio did not sleep beside Maria Inés that night, instead sitting upright against a tree where he had tethered his horse. Several of the Indians eyed his old mare with hunger, but they lacked the means to kill the animal and it was for this reason the animal remained alive when morning came.

The sun was nearly overhead when the horse began acting

strangely. Ygnacio tried to calm it, but it kept its head down as though listening to the earth. He pulled on the reata around its neck and still it refused to move. Irritated, he picked up a branch to lash it when the rumbling began.

Like a mighty waterfall, the sound raced toward them from the edge of the Yokut range where Fort Tejon had been built by the Americans to guard the pass from hostile Indians. The ripple of the earth caused some of the trees to lift slightly before settling back again. The shaking threw her to the ground. The horse reared and fought the rein until both horse and owner toppled to the ground. Maria Inés felt the land beneath her shuddering. The water in the river lifted and tossed fish far over the bank onto the sand. Where water had run, the flow disappeared underground and in its place quicksand bubbled in the streambed, leaving great depressions.

Maria Inés searched her basket for the sack of gold and when she found it she clasped it tightly. She saw that Ygnacio was not harmed, although the horse had wandered off in a confused manner. He ran after it. They could not afford to lose the animal.

Her husband returned many hours later with his head down. Maria Inés was busy drying three fish she had gathered from the sand. "Perhaps it will return on its own," she said as she laid one in her basket.

Ygnacio said nothing.

That night Maria Inés found her voice. "Without the horse, how are we to return to the rancho?" She hoped her husband would not hear the hopefulness behind her words. She remembered words spoken by Lacero's mother on the day he presented her as his wife.

"For our people, family is before anything else. Remember this and God will bless you."

Ygnacio looked out over the spilled waters of the creek. "We must eat the horse."

She realized the wisdom in his words. At the rancho they had enough to eat. And they were safe there, far from El Camino Real that brought trouble from the north and the south. But the hills were familiar here, even the air. Ygnacio knew this, too, because this was his land.

"Perhaps we find work with Señor Rios," she said. "They have moved to a new home after the murders, afraid for their safety living so close. Surely they need a couple who are hard workers."

Ignacio said nothing.

"After we find my son we will speak to Señor Rios."

She and Ygnacio agreed that they did not want to work the soil—they had no appetite for the work. She wanted to cook, for this is what she had done at the Mission and the work suited her. Her husband was no vaquero like Miguelito, intent instead to do the small duties, even to haul wood for her when she found work cooking for the ranchos in the busy seasons. He was not a light worker. His muscles were hard and tight, his mind hard as well, willing to do any job that would help him to provide for himself and his wife. She knew this about him, even though he never spoke the words.

Maria Inés found a position doing laundry for an American family for a few months before they gave up their claim and moved north to San Francisco. Before they left she reluctantly began speaking their language, words of "the devil's own language," even though the words grated in her ears. She worked hard from sunup to sundown, even after she caught her dress on fire from the open fire and burned her legs so badly that they were blistered. She kept her legs covered with aloe and a ragged skirt the woman salvaged from the rag pile as payment for her labor.

When the family moved on, she and Ygnacio found work at small ranchos, but each time the labor was hard and the pay was poor—usually only a place to sleep and a meal. When they asked for coin they were told that many other Indians were eager to have the work if they did not want it. Everywhere they looked they saw hunger walking in the bodies of people they recognized from the Missions. Some had scars or crippled limbs from work injuries. Others bore scabs or signs of illness. Some lay dying against the walls of the taverns in San Miguel or Pleyto, their bodies emaciated by drunkenness or the white man's diseases. Through all of this Maria Inés refused to touch the gold dust in her small sack.

"It belongs to my son. I will know when the time is right to give it to him."

Maria Inés watched her husband growing old with worry and she was afraid he would blame her for taking him away from the Villa Rancho where he had been happy. One day she said, "We will go back if you wish."

He was bent over a boot he was repairing for one of the vaqueros. It was not Miguelito's boot, for she watched the faces of the riders and she knew when he appeared, even though she was too shy to approach him. This was a stranger, a tough boy who carried a knife in his scabbard like a boast. The boot was worn through, but Ygnacio would make it like new with a few simple tools.

That night she prayed a rosary. As she fingered her beads she prayed, "Por favor, Blessed Mother, bring my son to me. Let him take me to his heart."

A few days later her husband returned from an errand carrying a small white goat that he tethered to a nearby willow. She saw it when she came out of the rancher's cookhouse to fetch a stack of wood and its innocence irritated her. "What have you brought us—a suckling? It is not yet old enough to be useful."

He looked up and his eyes smiled. "I found it wandering without a mother."

"So now we are ranchers?" she asked. "Or perhaps you mean to eat it."

"This one is female. We will find her a mate and she will provide meat for the table and milk for cheese."

She considered it for a moment. "It will have to sleep with us so it is not stolen."

"It will keep you warmer than *my* old bones."

She looked up and her tone was light. "We do not speak of dying."

The months passed. *The Time of the Troubles* was what the people called it when they spoke of it. Each day seemed harder than the one before. The rains fell hard for a solid winter, more rain than any of the people had ever seen. Rivers overflowed and no one could travel. Adobe houses with poor roofs melted and buildings crumbled with each new storm. Maria Inés brought the goat inside the poor shack she and Ygnacio made from oak branches and limbs they found in the forests to the west of the Salinas River. She tethered the goat nearby and it grazed the forest floor until it grew fatter than any of the native people. Throughout the valley people struggled in their willow huts and adobe shacks, waiting for the rains to cease and the mud to dry so they could hunt.

Finally the rains ended. The valleys grew thick with grass. The sheep multiplied, many ewes nursing triplets so that the shepherds had a hard time keeping track of their flocks. Cattle stolen from the Mission flocks grew fat and lazy with the easy life. Spring was a happy time when everyone celebrated their good fortune. Farmers rushed to plant their fields as soon as the soil was ready. They planted wheat and corn and fields of vegetables to fill their larders for the winter. Ygnacio found work harvesting, even though his wages were not paid at the end of the period and there was no one he could complain to.

The following year no rain fell at all. For an entire year the sun dried the land, producing no grass for the cattle. One day they watched as Señor Rios and his crew of vaqueros, Miguelito included, drove the last of the Mission cattle south to a place called Nipomo. The sound of hungry animals filled the air, pitiful sounds that interrupted sleep in the night. Ponds and streams dried up until farmers went to the river and chopped down the thirsty cottonwoods, sycamores, and willows so that ponds of brackish water would reappear.

Some of the ranchers near the great valley of the Tulare drove their cattle to the Sierra Nevada to summer in the mountains where there was still grass. Those who had no access to grass watched their cows eating pine boughs and sagebrush until even these disappeared and cattle began dropping, tongues swollen black from hunger and thirst. Women covered the ears of their children to block out the sounds of suffering. A few ranchers drove their cattle off of high cliffs to their deaths so they would not have to hear the sounds.

The land grew shadowed with the flight of condors feeding off the carcasses. Ranchers tried to save the pelts, but the cattle were too skinny and the hides were ruined. When the year was over, the ground was strewn with cattle skulls for as far as the eye could see.

One by one, ranchers began loading their wagons and departing. They had no heart to continue, some of them. Others lost their claim to the land because they could not pay their taxes and their land payments. Proud families were reduced to the level of their hired hands. But as always, it seemed as though the Indians suffered most.

"Where do we go, husband? Where do we find our place if this world does not have room for us?" Maria Inés watched the line of wagons heading north on El Camino Real.

Ygnacio sounded angry with her, but she knew he was only

frightened. "Where would you have us go? This is our home. We will stay here as our ancestors did. Where else is there to go?"

She bit her tongue. If he could speak with a brave heart, could she do otherwise? It was time to find her son and give him his inheritance. She hadn't seen him for many months, since the drought began and the fiestas and celebrations had ceased.

Maria Inés left her husband to his leather mending and took her basket to the dried river to dig for roots. Behind her, the goat bleated. They had eaten the old mother goat in the winter. The younger goat was big enough to survive on its own now. They would breed it soon and it would provide them with another goat and milk for cheese.

"When we find a place with steady work, maybe we will begin a flock," Ygnacio said.

She clutched the worn sack of gold inside her shawl and began following the trail to where a cluster of buildings had been built near the river. Ygnacio had built a camp on a rise where she could watch the vaqueros working the cattle. For three days the two of them remained, eating whatever they could find while she watched the fields, never taking her eyes off the trail in hopes of seeing a vaquero pass. One in particular caught her attention, a tall boy on a sorrel stallion. Each time he appeared she straightened and watched the direction in which he rode.

One evening she watched him ride to the ranch house and dismount. She began walking in that direction, glad Ygnacio remained behind with the goat because he understood this was hers to do alone.

The vaqueros had finished eating and were walking back to their horses when she stepped out from behind the adobe corral and gestured to her son. He looked up, surprised, and prepared to mount, but something in her eyes must have warned him because he waited until the others rode off before striding over to give her a disdainful frown.

"What do you want, squaw? Begging for a crumb? There is nothing here for you."

She pulled the sack from under her shawl and handed it to him.

"What is this, old woman? Some superstitious church beads for my soul?" His laugh was mocking and her heart bled for his blasphemy.

She had rehearsed her words a thousand times and they came out exactly as she intended. Perhaps it was the conviction in her voice that caused him to pause. Even if he hadn't, she would have spoken anyway.

"I buried your father in his fine boots because they were his pride. You will need a pair. And many silver conchos because you are a good man. Your father would agree." She took advantage of his hesitation to run her rough hand across his cheek before he flinched back in disgust. Her heart was light with happiness.

He opened the sack and his eyes widened when he saw what he held. From across the field one of the other riders whistled for him and he turned, his attention divided. When he looked up at her, his eyes were twin black pools of confusion.

She was afraid to spoil the moment, but she had carried the words on her tongue for many years. *"Amad a Dios, hijo."* Love God, son. The words of Padre Cabot. Her blessing finished, she stood silently and watched as he mounted his horse in a single leap and turned to race back to his friends.

Her walk back was made on the feet of a young girl. Happy images filled her mind and she thought of what she would tell her husband. How fine her son looked with his shiny black hair and his proud, dark eyes. His father was a handsome man and her son, also.

Ygnacio was waiting when she returned, a rabbit roasting on a willow stick he had hung between two small branches. That night they watched the stars and together they pointed out the bear and the dog in the heavens. When the stars were heavy above them, she slept beside her husband and thanked God for bringing him to her.

Grandmother appeared in a dream in which she pointed toward the east, to the land of the Tulare. When she woke, Maria Inés smiled at her husband and said, "My heart feels light this day. Let us make a new beginning."

Ygnacio nodded thoughtfully. "Someone will hire us because we know the land."

"My father was Yokut. From the long valley where the wild horses run."

Ygnacio turned to face east. "You are hungry for the taste of horsemeat?" he teased.

Maria Inés considered. "It is a long journey. We will die of hunger before we get half the way."

One day her husband returned to their camp. "I saw your son today," he said without looking up.

"Oh?" She waited to hear more, but she knew her husband.

In his own time he added, "He is a boy no longer. His jacket jingles with silver conchos. His bridle, as proud as any highborn Spanish caballero's."

She turned back to the string of garlic she was plaiting in order to hide her smile.

CHAPTER TWENTY-TWO

Ahead, a trio of vaqueros pushed a herd of horses across the Salinas. One of the men was Miguelito, his silver conchos shining in the sunlight. How handsome he looked, his face radiant with purpose. The two Americans who rode behind were lucky to have such a good rider. Maria Inés would like to tell them so, but she said nothing because it was not her place. And she did not speak English enough to say more than a few words.

One of the Americans, a leather-faced man with a dusty leather hat, drew his horse up and sat watching her. Her gathering forgotten, she clutched her threadbare shawl around her and hurried back to the camp where her husband waited. The man followed, in no apparent hurry. At the camp she slung her basket onto the ground and nervously tended to her pot, adding the roots to the thick stew already simmering. The man had caught the odors wafting from the pot because he drew up and called from the back of his horse, "You make a trade for some of that chow?"

She looked quickly at Ygnacio, who squatted on the ground weaving a lariat. After a moment her husband rose to his feet and said, "We will share what we have." His tone was nervous, she could tell, until the stranger reached into a small sack of silver. Her husband's eyes darkened at the three shining coins the man held out.

The man lifted his hand, five fingers widening. *"Cinco hombres."*

Ygnacio considered the food cooking in the pot and turned. She nodded just enough for him to understand—yes, there would be enough for five men—before he turned back to the man and nodded.

"*Gracias.*" The man lifted his hat to Maria Inés and wheeled his horse around. She began mixing the last of their cornmeal into a lump for tortillas. If the promise of payment was honored they would be able to buy corn for many days.

The men returned and squatted in the dirt, their spurs jingling with each movement. Maria Inés let the men dig the stew out of the pot with their tortillas. Clearly they had not eaten this day. They acted as though this was their last meal and there was none to come after this one. She looked at her son's downturned head, but she said nothing because she knew her greeting would not be welcome. She was surprised when he offered a quick, curious glance before he continued eating.

"I sorry I have no . . . thing more." She offered in halting English.

"Fine grub, Señora." When the man finished, he wiped his hands on his shirt and took the abalone cup of coffee she offered. The others would have to wait for their turn with the cup for she had only the one. He understood and sipped quickly before handing it back. When the meal was finished, he fished the three coins from his pocket and handed them to Ygnacio.

He walked over to where his American boss was preparing to mount, and the two of them spoke quietly. Soon he was back. He spoke to Maria Inés. "Say, don't 'spose you'd be wanting work?"

"Work, Señor?" The word was understood, but it had been many months since she had heard it.

"Sí. For Señor Nugent?"

Ygnacio stood twisting his hat in his gnarled hands. He glanced at her and his eyes were shamed the offer didn't include him. The American seemed to understand. He tilted his head in Ygnacio's direction.

"You do chores?"

"Sí, Señor."

He made a hoeing gesture. "Garden?"

"Sí, Señor."

He made a slashing motion against his arm. "Fix a feller up when he gets hurt?"

"Sí, Señor."

The man smiled and indicated their gear. "Think you could pack up, pronto?"

"Sí, Señor."

When the man left, Maria Inés filled her burden basket with their possessions and her husband filled his arms with what remained. She took the lead rope and tugged the goat forward. Soon they were walking toward a wagon piled high with more food and cooking implements than she had seen since the time of the padres. The camp wagon halted and the driver looked over at the two of them. "Climb in the back."

In the distance Miguelito rode point, driving the herd east toward the golden hills where the Yokuts once spent their winters. She drew her shawl around her shoulders and watched the golden grass passing under the wheels as the wagon cut a new trail in the earth.

"Where you go for the . . . ranch?" Ygnacio asked, his English halting and unsure.

"Valley east of here. Boss figures to set up a ranch in the Cholame."

Maria Inés heard the Indian word *Cholama*. In her dream, Grandmother had pointed toward such a land to the east. She turned and took a last long look at the Mission. For a moment her eyes were blinded by the glare of the sun on the water, its rays broken like the river itself in the dry season when the water ran beneath the earth, waiting for the rain.

She rode the rest of the way in silence, thinking of the things that had passed in her life and the things waiting. Beside her Ygnacio sat watching the land open out in front of him. A good day for beginning.

RECOMMENDED READING

If you wish to learn more, here is a list of books I used in my research. Many are available at Mission museum bookstores throughout the Central Coast of California.

Beebe, Rose Marie and Robert M. Senkewicz. *Testimonios.* Heyday Books: 2006.

Brusa, Betty War. *Salinan Indians of California.* Naturegraph: 1975.

Casey, Beatrice. *Padres and People of Old Mission San Antonio.* Casey Newspapers: 1976.

Coronel, Antonio, and Doyce Nunis, Jr. *Tales of Mexican California.* Bellerophon Books: 1994.

De La Pérouse, Jean François. *Life in a California Mission.* Heyday Books: 1989.

Hoffman, Lola B. *California Beginnings.* California State Department of Education: 1948.

Krieger, Dan. "Times Past" columns. *The Tribune:* 1985–2012.

MacLean, Angus. *From the Beginning of Time.* Padre Productions: 1985.

Margolin, Malcolm. *The Way We Lived.* Heyday Books: 1981.

Ohles, Wally. *The Lands of Mission San Miguel.* Word Dancer Press: 1997.

Oppel, Frank (Ed). *Tales of Old California.* Castle Books: 1989.

Taylor, Suzanne Pierce. *The Ancestors Speak.* Tesik: 2006

ABOUT THE AUTHOR

Anne Schroeder's childhood love of story was fueled by her Norwegian grandfather's tales of bandits in the Conejo Valley. She grew up on a sheep farm in Central California, graduated from college with a husband, toddler, and part-time job in the first wave of the Social Revolution, and considers life an adventure of small steps. Her passion for early California history has evolved into a multigenerational series about a Mission Indian family that includes *Maria Inés* and *Cholama Moon*.

Anne is current president of Women Writing the West and belongs to Western Writers of America and Native Daughters of the Golden West. Her fiction has won several awards. She resides in Southern Oregon with her husband, has three grown children, and writes about local history for Jefferson Public Radio. http://anneschroederauthor.blogspot.com www.facebook .com/anneschroederauthor.